REDHEADS
MEAN TROUBLE

And here's the proof—
plenty of trouble and an
excess of voluptuous redheads
in these hard-hitting capers
from the action-packed diary
of the private eye who likes
his cases hot and his
women warm.

Once again Johnny
Liddell steps into the ring
of the underworld, fighting
8 knockout rounds that pack
the toughest wallops
of his career.

FRANK KANE'S

STACKED DECK

WILDSIDE PRESS

contents

Dead Set

She wore a thin wisp of a bikini that was doing a half-hearted job of containing her full, tip-tilted breasts, a matching V of material was draped precariously high on her hips to converge between her thighs. Instead of concealing, the outfit had the effect of revealing.

Her hair was the color of a newly risen sun, complementing the icy blue of her eyes. Her sun-tanned face, free of any make-up, gleamed in the glaring sunshine, the bright red gash of her lips split occasionally to reveal the sparkling white of her teeth.

Johnny Liddell lounged in the chair alongside the pool, idly watched the effortless flow of her muscles as she worked her way down to him. Several times during her trip down the length of the pool she stopped to exchange a few words with some of the guests. Some he recognized from the regular appearances of their faces in movie magazines and Sunday supplements, some were more familiar to him from mugg shots in the various police files.

It was a typical Hollywood party.

Lydia Johnson was this year's Marilyn Monroe—a few years ago completely unknown, this year, by the alchemy of constant publicity, a sensation. The movie magazine that had failed to adorn its cover with her likeness during the past year was as rare as a war novel without four-letter words. The tilt of her breast was more familiar to the average American male than the name of the Secretary of State.

And she was in trouble.

Liddell waited until she had traversed the entire

length of the pool to where he sprawled, then swung his legs off the chair so she could sit down. From close, she smelled almost as good as she looked.

"Having fun?"

"That what I'm here for?" Liddell brought a pack of cigarettes from the pocket of his beach robe, shook two loose. He offered one to the girl, waited until she had fitted it between her lips and touched a match to it.

She took a long drag. The smoke dribbled from between half-parted lips. "Partly. But mostly because I need your help. I'm being blackmailed, Liddell, and I'm pretty sure the people behind it are here today." Her eyes finished their circuit of the pool, came back to his. "Meet me in the library in about twenty minutes. I'll tell you all about it."

Liddell lit his cigarette, blew the smoke upward in a feathery tendril. "Any idea which one in this mob scene is the heavy?"

The carrot-top replaced the fixed smile on her face, shook her head prettily. "Ideas, no proof. I can't talk about it any more right now. I'll see you inside." She took a last drag on the cigarette, ground it out in the tray next to the chair. "In twenty minutes."

Liddell lay back in the chair, watched the easy motion of the redhead's hips from the rear as she finished her tour of the guests.

He stood up, drew his beach robe tighter around his middle, walked down to where a foursome sat under a colored umbrella at a small, pool-side table.

The girls were standard products of the Hollywood glamour mill—blond, sleek, big-breasted and expensive-looking. The taller of the two men, in an open-necked sport shirt and fawn slacks, looked up as Liddell stopped at the table. His long black hair was split in a three-quarter part, slicked back over his head. His eyes were big, brown and liquid, his mouth petulant, with a slightly purple tinge. His eyes narrowed in surprise when he recognized Liddell.

"Look who's here, Angelo," he grunted to his short,

paunchier partner. "Liddell, the super snooper."

The man called Angelo rubbed the flat of his palm over the almost hairless pate of his head, scowled at the private detective. "Off your beat, ain't you, shamus? I thought we got rid of you when we shook the dust of 47th and Main off our shoes. What are you doing out here?"

Uninvited, Liddell pulled a chair from an adjoining table, dropped into it.

"Sit down," the paunchy man growled; "be my guest."

Liddell grinned at him and helped himself to a cigarette from the pack on the table. "So this is where you boys holed up after you left town?"

"Holed up?" Angelo growled. "What kind of holed up? Me and the kid here, we figure business is moving west so we move with it." He turned to the girls. "You kids run along for a few minutes. We got a lot of old times to talk over with the shamus here."

With obvious appreciation, he watched the rear view as the girls scampered toward the bar at the far end of the pool and returned his attention to Liddell with reluctance.

"One thing I got to say for you, shamus. You travel first class. This Lydia Johnson broad, this is nothing but the best. This year."

Liddell nodded. "A nice piece of goods," he conceded. "She sure came up in a hurry. Who's behind her?"

Angelo shrugged his shoulders, looked to the moist-eyed man on his left. "You hear something about someone being behind the Carrot Top, Marty?" When the sleek-haired man pursed his lips, shook his head, Angelo turned back to Liddell. "We don't hear nothing about this, Liddell. So maybe nobody's behind her. The broad's got talent sticking out all over her. You can see that. No?" He exposed dingy teeth in a lewd smile. "Real talent."

Liddell's eyes hopscotched around the pool. "I see

a few of the other boys around. Eddie Match, Leo Sullivan. Sort of an Old Home Week?"

Angelo swabbed at the light film of perspiration on his forehead with the back of a hairy hand. "Like I said, shamus, all the action is out here these days. The Big Town's got nothing left for a guy who likes to live good. This is the life—plenty broads, plenty sunshine. A man gets used to living like this real easy. Right, Marty?"

Marty bobbed his head obediently. "Right, Ange."

Angelo broke off at a signal from Marty, turned to greet an overdressed female of indeterminate age who was flouncing from table to table. When she approached their table, it was evident that a heavy make-up job was fighting a losing battle with wrinkles and crow's feet.

"Angelo, I just wanted to tell you we dropped by your place in the Valley last night. Divine, my dear, absolutely divine. Catch my 11:15 broadcast tonight, I'm sure you'll be delighted with what I have to say about it." She eyed Liddell curiously. "Another of your colleagues? I can see he's from back East by his complexion."

"Just a character I knew in the Big Town, Laura. Liddell make the acquaintance of Miss St. Clair. What she don't know about this town ain't worth knowing. Ain't that right, Marty?"

Marty went through the necessary head-bobbing motions.

"I've heard your broadcasts and I've read your columns, Miss St. Clair," Liddell told her. "I'm glad to meet you."

"Angelo, you disappoint me," the faded woman scolded. "Here I thought all your friends were characters and you spring a straight man on me. Actually speaks English."

"You meet all kinds," the stocky man grunted. "Besides, Liddell ain't a friend in a strict manner of speaking. He's a shamus I used to run into back East once in a while."

The columnist's eyes were alive and interested behind the enameled façade of her make-up. "A shamus? That's a private detective, isn't it?" She dropped her voice, lowered her face conspiratorially. "Have you got something juicy for Laura, Mr. Liddell? The boys will tell you I always protect a source—and I pay well for exclusives."

Liddell shook his head. "Sorry to disappoint you, but I'm not working. Just taking a breather before going back East. I haven't been doing anything more glamorous than tracking down a movie-struck kid—"

The columnist's eyes narrowed. "But you rated an invitation to a Lydia Johnson party. Possibly you knew her before she became a star? Tell me, Liddell, is it true that—"

Liddell took a last drag on his cigarette, made a production of crushing it out. "As a matter of fact, I just happened to meet her through a mutual friend. She mentioned the party and it sounded like a nice way to kill an afternoon."

The columnist managed to look miffed. "Possibly you think it's none of my business?" Before Liddell could answer, she snapped, "Everything that happens in this town is my business. If you did have anything on the fire, or if you hope to do any business in this town, you might find it worthwhile to co-operate with Laura." Her eyes flicked to the other two at the table and back. "Most people do." She nodded to Angelo and Marty, flounced on to the next table.

"You used to get along good with the press." Marty grinned, when the woman was out of earshot. "You're sure losing your touch."

"A dame like that's not the press. She's a walking scandal factory." Liddell checked his wristwatch. "I know it will break you all up, but I'm going to have to tear myself away."

"I'll live," Angelo grunted.

Liddell skirted the other tables that lined the pool,

headed for the portable bar at the end. He ordered a Smirnoff and tonic, watched while the man in the white jacket made a big deal of tilting the vodka bottle over the ice cubes. Back at the table he had just left, Angelo and Marty had their heads together. Angelo was doing most of the talking, Marty's head bobbing in agreement.

The private detective finished his drink, set the glass down on the bar, wandered toward a set of french windows that led into a small playroom. The air in here was cool, fragrant. He crossed the playroom to a door that opened on a larger room that was half library, half den.

2

Lydia Johnson had draped a chenille robe around her, sat huddled in a comfortable looking overstuffed library chair. She had a tall drink in her hand that clinked when she waved to Liddell.

"Close the door so we won't be disturbed." When he had swung the door shut behind him, she waved to the built-in bar. "Help yourself."

"Met a couple of old friends while I was waiting," he told her while he spilled some Smirnoff into a glass, dumped in some ice and washed it down with tonic. "Angelo Russo and his yes-man Marty. They introduced me to a she-vulture named Laura St. Clair."

"That woman gives me the willies. Always prying."

Liddell took his drink, crossed the room to a chair facing her. "A couple of other guests interested me. Eddie Match and Leo Sullivan. Quite a select crew."

The redhead shrugged. "Everybody out here knows Angelo. He runs one of the best gambling traps out here. Everybody who counts gives the place a big play." She swirled the liquid around in her glass. "Eddie Match is a big agent out here these days. Didn't you know that?"

Liddell grunted. "The only thing I ever heard of Match agenting was a stag or a smoker."

"He still peddles flesh, but he gets paid better for it these days." She ran her fingers through her hair, brushed it back from her forehead. "Liddell, I'm going to lay all the cards on the table. Back before I hit the big time, I did some work for Eddie Match."

Liddell took a deep sip from his glass, waited.

"Now that I'm on top, it's popped up to louse me up. Bad."

"What is it? Pictures?"

The girl got up, walked to the desk, took a key from the top drawer. She moved back an oil painting, revealing a wall safe. She used the key, opened the safe, dug into its interior. When she turned around she had two envelopes in her hand. She walked over, tossed them into Liddell's lap.

"You'll have to remember that I was just a kid. And hungry." She walked to the window, pulled back the drape and stared out across the well-kept lawn while he opened the first envelope.

It was a manuscript titled "When Lydia Johnson Was a Call Girl—She Was the 'Specialty' of the House." Liddell skimmed through the article, growled deep in his throat.

"They want you to pay off on this? They're nuts. Nobody would touch this thing with a six-foot pole."

"You'd better take a look at the art to illustrate it. In the other envelope." She didn't turn from the window.

Liddell dumped a batch of 4 x 5 prints from the other envelope, flipped through them, whistled soundlessly.

"You must have been more than hungry to pose for pix like these. You must have been nuts."

"They weren't posed. We did a show sometimes— they must have been shot then." She let the drape fall back into place, turned around. "All right, they have me cold. I don't know how much they want, they haven't set the figure yet." She picked up a cigarette from the table, stuck it between her lips, smoked with short, angry puffs. "I'll go for the payoff because I have no choice. That's what I need you for, Liddell. I want you to make the payoff. But I want to make sure it's a one-time deal."

Liddell returned the prints to the envelope, read through the article more carefully. "You said you have no idea who's behind this?"

"An idea. No proof." The cigarette drooped from the corner of her mouth when she talked. "Eddie Match booked those shows, and, while he never showed up personally, Leo Sullivan was always front row center."

"Angelo fit in the picture?"

"I think so. I've been taking a good look at those pictures. Don't those decorations in the room look familiar?"

Liddell grinned. "I hadn't noticed. You kept getting in the way."

"Well, I did. I'm positive those pictures were taken in the private room on the third floor of the place Angelo used to run on 47th Street when he was operating in New York."

"Then any one of them could have arranged for the pictures to be taken. Anybody else here at the party?"

The redhead rubbed the outside of her arms as though to massage some warmth into them. "They're the only ones out there that I know have any idea I was a call girl."

Liddell tossed the envelopes on an end table. "I don't know if paying off is a good idea, baby. You can never be sure it's the last installment. There are plenty of ways to pull a double cross."

"I've got to take that chance. If I don't, and that manuscript falls into the hands of a scandal magazine, they'd have a picnic with it. And if they've got those pictures to back it up, I couldn't even open my mouth." She chain-lit a fresh butt, dropped into the chair dispiritedly. "This is no nude calendar or leg art, mister. If this gets out, I'm through for good."

"And if you start paying off, you may be hooked for good. Your only out is for us to find out who has the negatives and any other prints and discourage them."

The girl licked at her lips. "You think you could?"

"It's worth a try."

The redhead got up from her chair, walked over to where he stood, laid her hand on his arm. "Look, Liddell, I'm not putting on the wronged innocence act. Those are pictures of me and, while I'm not proud of them, I'm not yelling frame. I'm just asking to be let off the hook."

"Don't worry, baby, I'm almost shockproof. Making a living that way isn't an easy way to keep groceries on the table, that's for sure. But it's a much more honest living than the guy who tries to bleed you for those groceries."

Her hand tightened on his arm. "I don't have to tell you how grateful I'll be for anything you can do."

"What's the best time to see Angelo at his place?"

"Eleven, eleven-thirty. You've got plenty of time."

Liddell reached over, kissed the half-open lips. They were soft, moist. She melted against him, held him close. After a moment, he drew back.

"What about your guests?"

The redhead shrugged. "You know Hollywood parties. As long as the liquor holds out, they don't care if they never see the sucker that's lifting the tab."

Liddell reached down caught her lightly in his arms, walked toward the couch. The robe fell open. The brown of her body was criss-crossed by two contrasting white strips outlining the shape of the bikini.

3

Johnny Liddell took the coastal highway south, a tortuous route that seemed to hug the shoreline most of the way. Somewhere beyond the black abyss that yawned off to the right there was a rumble of surf and the hissing sound of water retreating from the beach.

When his headlights picked out the brass sign announcing *Angelo's* he swung off the macadam through two large stone pillars onto a crushed bluestone driveway which wound and curved its way through a row of trees to the house.

Angelo's turned out to be a sprawling old building that looked like any old home that had been kept up. Shrubs and lawns seemed to be in good condition, and the house itself was bathed in the glow of hidden spotlights. He pulled up to the canopied entrance, turned the rented car over to a uniformed attendant.

The main hall of the place was filled with small groups of patrons, mostly in evening dress. Overhead, a pall of smoke stirred restlessly in the breeze from the opened door.

Off to the left, one of the original parlors had been converted into a lounge with a bar running the length of one wall. Liddell ambled in, found himself some elbow room at the bar.

He ordered a bourbon on the rocks, turned his back to the bar and looked around. To judge by the number of reel-life faces he recognized in the place, Angelo had obviously become well accepted by the movie colony. When the bartender slid the drink across to him. Liddell dropped a five on the bar.

"Angelo show yet?"

The bartender raised his eyebrows. "Mr. Angelo is here every night, sir. You a friend of his?"

Liddell nodded. "From New York. Name's Liddell."

The bartender picked up the bill from alongside the drink, shuffled to the far end of the bar, rang it up. He was back in a moment with the change. Liddell gave no sign that he saw when the barman a few minutes later picked up a phone from under the bar, muttered a few words into it.

Liddell was just on the verge of ordering a refill

when a two-hundred-pound fashion plate in a mid-night-blue tuxedo, sporting a red carnation in his buttonhole, sidled up to him. "Mr. Liddell?"

Liddell nodded.

"Mr. Angelo will see you in his office." The way Blue Tuxedo said it, it sounded like getting invited into Mr. Angelo's office was like getting a free pass from St. Peter. "If you'll just come this way."

The office was at the end of the corridor leading off the entrance hall. The man in the tuxedo rapped on a door stenciled *Private* and waited. After a moment, it was opened by Marty, who dismissed the man in the tuxedo with a nod.

The room beyond was comfortably furnished with large, easy chairs, a few tables scattered around. The illumination was provided entirely by lamps, giving the room a warm, intimate glow.

Angelo was sprawled in an easy chair, his feet propped up on a low table. He watched Liddell enter with no show of enthusiasm. Somewhere a radio was spilling soft dance music into the room.

"I thought we said good-by at the pool this afternoon, shamus," he growled. "We figured you'd be on your way back East by now. Didn't we, Marty?"

Marty, leaning against the door, nodded.

"You didn't think I'd leave without coming out to take a look at your place, did you?"

Angelo reached into a humidor and brought up a cigar. He bit off the end, spat it at the waste basket. "Okay, so now you seen it."

Liddell grinned. "You know, Angelo, it's like you said. This place grows on you. I might stay a while."

The man in the chair stuck the unlit cigar in his mouth, rolled it in the center of his lips between thumb and forefinger. "This ain't your kind of town, Liddell. I don't think the climate would agree with you."

The radio started spouting a commercial.

"You seem to be thriving," Liddell walked over to

the humidor, selected a cigar, held it to his nose, then dropped it back in the box.

Angelo scowled at him. "You and me, we're two different kinds of guys. Me, I keep my nose out ·of other people's business. Like that, like you say, a guy could thrive in this climate." He chewed on his cigar reflectvely. "Only you never learned how to do that."

"Sounds dull."

Angelo stretched his feet out, contemplated the high gloss on his shoes. "So you figure you're tough, you can't get hurt. But sometimes when people blow the whistle, they're the ones get hurt."

"You mean my client might get hurt if I don't lay off?"

The man in the chair pulled the cigar from between his teeth, examined the soggy end, pasted a stray leaf back with the tip of his tongue. "Who even knew you had a client?" His eyes rolled up from the cigar to Liddell. "I'm just saying it never did pay to run and yell copper. Even to a shamus. It could make a guy real unpopular."

"A guy?"

Angelo shrugged. "Or a doll. There are guys get their kicks working over dolls. To them, guys or dolls, it don't make no difference. That's the way they get their kicks."

"Like Leo Sullivan?"

"Why don't you ask Leo?"

The announcer on the radio boomed, "—and here she is, the Boswell of the Hollywoods, that see-all, know-all, tell-all reporter, Laura St. Clair." There was a brief fanfare of canned music, then the cloying voice of the columnist filled the room.

Angelo held his hand up. "Just a minute. She's supposed to give the joint a plug tonight. I want to hear it."

He sat, the unlit cigar clenched between his teeth, nodding his head in obvious agreement while the voice on the radio drooled superlatives about his operation.

When she finally switched to another subject, Angelo signaled to Marty.

"Not a bad plug. But turn her off. That voice of hers gives me bumps." He turned his attention back to Liddell. "I'm going to give you some advice for free, shamus. Don't crowd us. We don't want no trouble out here, but if we got to have trouble we know how to handle it. Right, Marty?"

The other man's head bobbed obediently.

"Okay, as long as we're giving out with the free advice—me, I get nervous when anybody crowds a client of mine. Real nervous. And when I get nervous, somebody gets hurt."

The man in the chair swung his feet off the low table, they hit the floor with a thud. "You're threatening Angelo?" He hit his chest with the back of his hand. He got up, walked over to Liddell, stuck his face so close the private detective could smell the garlic on his breath. "Nobody comes into my joint to threaten Angelo."

Liddell studied the club man's face. The years away from New York had made a lot of changes in Angelo, Liddell realized. The wolfishness of his face was blurred by a soft overlay of fat. Flat, lusterless eyes still peered from under heavily veined, thickened eyelids, but the soft pouches under them took away the old menace.

Liddell put his hand against the stocky man's chest and shoved. Angelo reeled backwards; the low table caught him behind the knees, dumped him in a tangle of arms and legs on the floor.

Marty's hand dipped into his pocket, reappeared with an open switchblade. He shuffled toward Liddell flat-footedly, the blade of the knife upward in the approved knife fighter fashion.

"You're pushing your luck too far, snooper," he growled.

He circled the private detective warily for a moment, then made a sudden lunge. Liddell side-stepped, caught his wrist as the knife whizzed past and twisted.

Marty screamed with pain, spun through the air and landed in a heap at Liddell's feet, the knife skidding across the floor. The private detective reached down, caught a handful of Marty's hair and pulled him to his feet. He sank his left to the cuff in the other man's midsection, chopped viciously at the side of his ear. Marty hit the floor face first, and didn't move.

Liddell walked over to where the knife lay, picked it up, tested the point on the ball of his thumb. He turned to where Angelo was painfully pulling himself to his feet.

"We're not saying we're not in the market to buy," Liddell grunted. "But like they say in the ads—all sales are final."

Angelo's eyes hopscotched sullenly from the knife to Liddell's face and back. "We've got nothing to sell but grief, shamus." He nodded to where Marty lay. "In your case, Marty's liable to want to make it real cheap. Even give it away."

Liddell stepped across the prostrate form of Marty, knife in hand. As he neared Angelo, the club man flattened back against the wall.

"Wait a minute, Liddell, don't do anything crazy. I told you I got nothing to sell." The perspiration was glistening on his upper lip, beads were forming on his forehead. "That's not my line. You know that. I got wheels and the tables downstairs. That's plenty for me."

"Whose line is it, Angelo?"

The stocky man licked at his lips. "I don't stool."

Liddell touched the point of the blade to the soft fat that hung under the other man's neck, nicked the skin. Angelo grunted, touched his finger to the nick, brought away a drop of blood.

"Who's selling?"

"Maybe a buy isn't what's up. Maybe nobody's selling."

Liddell scowled. "You trying to tell me something?"

The club operator shook his head. "I'm not telling you anything. You figure it out for yourself. How much can a real operator get from a take on the black? Two, three, maybe five gees tops? A dame that's the hottest property in town right now under a management contract is good for twenty times that. Maybe more."

Liddell lowered the knife. "So that's the gimmick. The shake is just the softener-upper?"

"You didn't get that from me, shamus, I'm no stool."

Liddell grinned at him. "You could fool me."

4

Lydia Johnson was sitting by the pool when Johnny Liddell returned to her place in Beverly Hills. She wore a light-blue dressing gown that made it highly debatable that she wore anything under it. She listened to Liddell's report on the interview with Angelo and frowned.

"Eddie Match?" She chewed on the end of a highly shellacked nail, considered it. "Then it won't be money they'll want, it'll be a management contract."

Liddell sat on the end of the chair, nodded. "That's the way it sounds. What kind of a stable does Match have anyway?"

"A lot of big names. He keeps adding all the time." The frown between the girl's eyes grew deeper. "You think that's the way he gets all his clients? By blackmail?"

Liddell shrugged. "I don't know how else a pimp could get to be a top talent agent so quickly otherwise."

The girl winced at the word "pimp." She reached for a cigarette, tapped it on the arm of the chair. "One way or another it looks like I'm cut out to peddle my wares for Eddie Match, doesn't it?"

"How about your studio? Would they stand up if there was a showdown and those pictures were circulated?"

"I don't know. They've got an awful lot invested in me, but I don't know if they could afford to stand up against that kind of a blast." She lit the cigarette, blew twin streams through her nostrils. "I'm over a worse barrel than I thought. I guess I've just wasted your time, Liddell. This isn't going to be a single payoff deal. It looks like I'm hooked from here on in."

Liddell growled deep in his chest. "Maybe not. I still haven't had a talk with Match. Maybe I can persuade him to be nice."

"Nobody, but nobody, talks Eddie Match out of a buck."

"You'd be surprised how persuasive I can be." Liddell reached over, took a drag from her cigarette. "Where's the best place to run into him?"

"He has an office on Sunset. Near La Cienaga. But I don't imagine it will do any good." She reached over, crushed out her cigarette "I don't suppose you heard Laura St. Clair's broadcast tonight?"

"About Angelo's?" Liddell grinned. "What a drool."

The redhead shook her head. "I mean about you."

Liddell scowled. "About me?" He shook his head. "Angelo turned it off right after the plug for his joint. What about me?"

Lydia shrugged. "Oh, she didn't mention you by name, but she warned one of the big studios that one of its stars was flirting with bad headlines by getting mixed up with a notorious private eye. She meant me—and you. By tomorrow, the eager beavers from the studio's publicity department will be begging Laura for details and you'll be ruled off the track."

"That gives us tomorrow to work on Eddie Match."

"You're still game? Laura can throw an awful lot of weight around. She can ruin you in this town. At least in my case the studio will try to protect an investment."

"Like I said, we still have tomorrow."

The redhead stared at him, grinned. "And tonight."

She stood up, there was a soft rustle as she slid the gown back over her shoulders. Her body gleamed in the reflected light, the white strips of untanned skin in sharp contrast to the darkness of her body. Her legs were long, sensuously shaped. Full rounded thighs swelled into high-set hips, converged into a narrow waist. Her breasts were full and high, their pink tips straining upward.

"How about a swim?" Her body flashed toward the water, arched gracefully, then disappeared with a splash.

Johnny Liddell grinned, watched until the girl's head broke the water. She flattened out on her back, beckoned to him invitingly. He kicked off his loafers, started tugging at his tie.

5

At eleven the next morning, Johnny Liddell stepped out of a cab outside a white stucco four-story building on Sunset just off La Cienaga. The air was super-heated and dry from the beaming sun. He pushed through the glass doors, soaked up the coolness of the air-conditioning.

The directory in the vestibule offered the information that Edward Match Co., Artists' Representatives, occupied Suite 406. He headed for the one-cage elevator in the rear of the lobby.

On the fourth floor, he plowed through a runner of thick red carpet to the front suite in the building. The reception room was empty except for a girl with patently bleached hair who presided over a switchboard behind a railing that cut the room in two. On the walls, giant-sized photographs of top Hollywood stars, presumably Match clients, were recessed in indirectly lighted frames.

Liddell crossed to the railing. The blonde looked up at him with no show of enthusiasm; she didn't miss a beat on her gum.

"I want to see Match. The name's Liddell."

The girl jabbed at her hair with the tips of her fingers. "Do you have an appointment?"

Liddell grinned, looked around the empty office. "You kidding?"

The girl at the switchboard appeared not to hear. "I'll see if he can see you." She stabbed at a key, murmured into her headphone. She flicked the key upward. "He'll see you."

Eddie Match sat perched on the corner of a highly polished desk that dominated the private office. The end of a toothpick protruded from the corner of his mouth; his eyes were half-lidded disks of expressionless gray slate. He waited while Liddell closed the door behind him, rolled the toothpick from one side of his mouth to the other.

"Long time no see," Liddell nodded.

"Couldn't be too long." Match was lean, affected carefully tailored suits that showed a complete understanding with his tailor. His hair was beginning to gray, was worn in a closely clipped crew cut. "What's on your mind?"

"Lydia Johnson."

Match pulled the toothpick from between his teeth, studied the macerated end incuriously. "So?"

"She's a client. I'm just passing word around that I don't like my clients leaned on."

The lean man rolled his eyes upward from the toothpick to Liddell. "Meaning?"

"Somebody's trying to hustle my client, Match. Somebody who knows her from the old days, somebody who has a batch of pictures to prove it. I understand there's a price tag on them. We'll go for a price tag, but with no strings."

"I don't make you, Liddell. I do know this. If your client wants to get back those pictures, sending a shamus around to throw muscle isn't the way to do it." He chewed on the toothpick. "If I were handling her—"

"Which you're not."

Match permitted himself a thin-lipped smile around the toothpick. "You never know in this town do you, peeper?" He watched Liddell make himself comfortable in a leather armchair. "Like I said, if I was handling her, maybe I could make a deal with the people who have the pictures."

"I like my way better," Liddell grunted.

The lean man shook his head. "You're playing out of your league. This isn't New York, where you get a lot of things solved with a .45. This is Hollywood where who you know gets you what you want."

"Maybe I can take a quick course in how to make friends."

Match flipped the toothpick at the waste basket. "You're a little late. Nobody in this town would touch you with a six-foot pole. Maybe you don't listen to Laura St. Clair. But everyone else in this town does."

"She put the finger on me, eh?"

The lean man shrugged. "It figures. Nobody wants to cross Laura by playing ball with a guy who heads her list. The studio finds out she's talking about Lydia Johnson, they bend over backwards to make sure Lydia stays on the right side of St. Clair. The studio's got too much dough tied up in Johnson to let her louse herself up." He hopped off the desk, walked over to the water cooler, helped himself to a cup of water. "Who knows what'll happen when they find out how she made her bread and butter in the old days? A smart agent might be able to keep them from doing something rash—like throwing her out on her can."

"You mean a retired pimp? Or have you retired, Match?"

The color drained from the agent's face. Little lumps formed on his jaw at the corners of his mouth. "I don't have to take that kind of talk from you, peeper. You've been pushing your luck ever since you got into this town. Maybe you'll push it too far." .

"Why tell me? Why don't you tell that other important friend of yours? The peeper—Leo Sullivan. Maybe he'll do something about it. Or was he only handy with girls?"

"I'll tell him you were asking."

"Yeah. Do that. I'd hate to go back to New York without a chance to see him."

Match's grin was bleak, strained. "Don't worry. You will."

6

Johnny Liddell leaned on the bar with the ease of long experience, made overlapping circles with the wet bottom of his glass. He checked his watch for the third time, growled under his breath.

He could tell the minute Lydia Johnson entered the bar by the hush that fell over the bar and the adjoining tables. As she walked toward him, the entire room seemed to be releasing its collective breath.

She moved in beside him at the bar. "Am I very late?"

Liddell grinned at her. "Late enough."

The Carrot Top ordered a vodka Gibson, pouted at Liddell. "Where have you been all afternoon? I thought you'd come back to my place after you saw Match."

"I've been to the library." He dropped his voice, looked around. "Let's sit down. I think I'm on to something." He indicated an end table to the bartender, led the girl over.

"I've been reading Laura St. Clair's columns in the files. You read them?"

The redhead shrugged, sipped at her drink. "Everyone out here does. It's required reading. Laura packs a lot of weight in this town. She's been out here almost as long as Louella and longer than Hopper."

"You notice how often she uses blind items? Like what well-known star's career will be ruined by this scandal or that scandal?"

"They all do. It protects them from a libel action for one thing. For another, it prevents innocent people from getting hurt."

"I wonder how many of those blind items made sense to Eddie Match's clients?"

The girl stopped with the glass halfway to her lips. "I don't get it."

"Look, someone has been softening up these big names so Match could move in and slough them with that representation deal. How else would a character like Match latch onto so many top clients? And at that rate?"

"You think Laura's mixed up in a shakedown racket?"

"And what a racket. Instead of taking peanuts for payoffs, they take over management of top stars and have a gold mine for life."

Lydia caught her lower lip between her teeth, worried it. "Even if you were right? How do you go about proving it?"

"If I'm right, she must have some of the material in her files." He pulled an envelope from his breast pocket, consulted penciled notes on the back. "I jotted down six of Match's clients. I'm going to check and double-check her files on them. If I'm right, she'll have something on each of them."

"And me?"

Liddell grinned. "Before I even start checking the rest, I'll find her folder on you and burn it. You're my client. Remember?"

The redhead covered his hand with hers, squeezed. "Be careful, Johnny. It's awful risky." She looked around, made certain no one was within hearing distance. "When do you intend to do it?"

"What time is she on the air?"

"Eleven-fifteen to eleven-thirty every week day."

Liddell winked. "By tomorrow the studio may be putting the heat on you to unload me. Tonight's our only chance. Keep your fingers crossed."

Laura St. Clair had a combination office and apartment in the penthouse of a pile of concrete and plate
glass that towered over Wilshire Boulevard.

Johnny Liddell dropped his cab a block away and
took his time ambling toward the entrance. The doorman pushed open the heavy glass door, eyed Liddell incuriously, and forgot him a moment later running to
open the door of a cab.

Inside the lobby, Johnny Liddell headed for the
bank of elevators in the rear. He avoided the cage
marked *Penthouse,* stepped into one of the others.
"Ten, please," he told the bored operator.

The cage whirred softly upward, slid to a smooth
stop at the tenth floor. Liddell got out, headed for the
front of the building. When the doors of the elevator
clanged behind him, he reversed his direction and
headed for a door at the rear marked *Stairway.* He
climbed the remaining nine flights to the penthouse.

On the staircase he checked his watch. Eleven-ten.
Five minutes before Laura St. Clair went on the air
to bring her palpitating audience up to date on the
doings of the stars. At this moment, Laura St. Clair
would be at her mike, checking over her script for the
last time before the "On the Air" signal flashed. He
estimated that he had a minimum of half to three-quar-
ters of an hour to find what he was looking for.

He listened outside the penthouse door for a moment, then brought a fine, thin rule from his pocket
and fitted it to the door. On the second try he was re-
warded by a sharp click and the knob turned in his
hand. He opened the door, slipped in and closed it
behind him.

He waited in the dark for a moment while his eyes
adjusted themselves. Then he brought out a fountain-
pen light, pierced the darkness with its beam. The
room he was in seemed to be a sort of reception room.
Two doors led off it in opposite directions. Cautiously,
he made his way to one of the doors, pushed it open.
It was a small workroom with a cluttered desk, a few

filing cabinets and a bank of telephones. He walked to the desk, snapped on a small desk radio, turned it low to the station on which Laura St. Clair broadcast. He caught the closing commercial of the program preceding hers.

By the shaded light of the desk lamp, carefully, methodically, Liddell sifted through the papers on the columnist's desk, then turned his attention to the drawers, found nothing of interest.

There was the sound of three chimes from the radio. Then, an unctuous voice flowed through to announce:

"And now, through the courtesy of Petal, the cream that gives your skin the glow of roses, we bring you that chatterbox of Hollywood, the woman who knows everything about the people you dream about—Miss Laura St. Clair, our see-all, hear-all and tell-all reporter ..."

Liddell closed his ears to the monotonous patter of the announcer, turned his attention to the filing cabinets. He checked the folder on Lydia Johnson, found the usual innocuous studio biography, a few typed items, obviously from her press agent. The files of the other six names, the names of Eddie Match's clients, were equally innocuous. Liddell growled under his breath, looked around for the possible hiding place for the kind of explosive material contained in the blackmail piece on Lydia Johnson.

Foot by foot he examined the paneling of the wall. A section behind the desk gave off a hollow sound. He put his head close to it, rapped it again, grunted his satisfaction. There was a hollow space behind the paneling. A careful search of the entire surface revealed a cleverly disguised button on the baseboard. When he pressed on it, the entire section of paneling slid back. A small, squat filing cabinet was contained in the space behind the wall.

He pulled open the drawer, fumbled through the folders, came up with one marked *Lydia Johnson*. Inside it were the originals and negatives of the photos he had seen in the girl's home.

Laura St. Clair's voice sounded louder than it had, intruding itself on Liddell's consciousness. He turned back to the radio. It was still a low mumble.

Then Laura St. Clair said again, in a loud tone, "Don't move."

7

Liddell started, looked to the door, where the columnist stood covering him with a businesslike looking automatic. He looked from her to the radio and back.

"You don't know much about radio technique, do you, Liddell? We do our east coast broadcast at 7:15 to allow for the difference in time. Then, very often, we do the west coast rebroadcast from tape." The gun in her hand was steady. "I did underestimate you, though. How'd you tumble to what we were doing?"

Liddell shrugged. "That article you used to shake Johnson with. It was a real pro job. Neither Match nor Russo could have written it and they certainly wouldn't cut some hack writer in on it. That plus the fact that someone with real pull was herding the clients into Match's agency."

The columnist waved him away from the desk with the snout of the gun. "Now you're a real problem," she sighed. "I can't very well have you running around knowing what you do, can I?"

Liddell shrugged. "You could shoot me while I was trying to take the gun away from you. That's always a good one."

The woman considered, shook her head. "There might be too many questions. No, I guess it will have to be some place away from here. As far as possible." She waved the gun at the far wall. "Walk over to that wall. Keep your hands where I can see them." She followed him to the blank wall with the snout of the gun. "Stand about an arm's length away, then lean forward on tiptoe and support yourself against the wall with your fingertips."

Liddell leaned forward, supported himself with his fingertips. While he was off balance, the woman walked up behind him, slid her arm around him and tugged his .45 from its holster.

"How long do I stand like this?"

The woman laughed. "Not too long. I'm going to have somebody come over for you." He could hear her at the telephone as she tapped the cross bar. "Helene? Miss St. Clair. You know that little arrangement I have for smuggling in my contacts without anybody seeing them? That's right. Have the penthouse elevator left at the basement level." She listened for a moment. "No, that'll be all right. My visitor will leave the same way. You can have the cage left in the basement overnight. I won't be using it again tonight. Thank you, my dear." She dropped the receiver on its hook. "Any questions, Liddell?"

The private detective shook the perspiration out of his eyes and swore.

The woman chuckled, dialed a number. "Leo? This is St. Clair. You'd better come over to my place right away." There was a brief pause. "I don't care how busy you are. I came back to my place unexpectedly and found your friend Liddell going through my files." She waited a moment. "That's right. Liddell. How soon?" She grunted her assent. "The penthouse elevator will be at the basement level. Don't let anyone see you coming up here." She dropped the receiver on its hook.

Liddell tried to blink the blinding stream of perspiration from his eyes. The ache in his fingers had translated itself to his arms and shoulders. He took it as long as he could, then his knees threatened to give way under him. He managed to hold out for another three minutes, then his knees folded, dumping him into a heap on the floor.

"Not bad," Laura St. Clair grunted. "You lasted

almost five minutes. Three is par for the course."

Liddell managed to get one lead-heavy arm to his face, swabbed at the perspiration that glistened on it. He watched while she screwed a cigarette into a holder, tilted it in the corner of her mouth and touched a match to it. The gun was never more than inches away from her hand.

"If you're thinking of trying anything, Liddell"— she blew smoke at him—"forget it. By the time you got the knots out of your legs, you'd never make it."

She was on her second cigarette when there was a cautious knock on the door.

"Come on in. It's open," she called.

Leo Sullivan was tall, heavy-set, his shoulders stooped so that his hands seemed to dangle in apelike nearness to his knees. His low hairline, the coarseness of his black hair and the tufts that stuck out of his nostrils and ears added to the apelike effect. He grinned when he saw Liddell on the floor, his back against the wall.

"Eddie Match says you been asking about me, shamus." He walked over, caught Liddell by the hair, pulled him to his feet.

The private detective's legs felt as though they had been transfused with red-hot lead. His knees showed signs of an inability to support his weight. He stood swaying, his face glistening with perspiration.

"That's quite a parlor trick Laura has, eh, shamus?" He turned his attention to the woman. "You got his gun?"

Laura nodded, pulled open her desk drawer, took out the .45. She handed it over to the apelike man. "You got a car?"

Sullivan nodded, hefted the .45 in the palm of his hand. "Nice iron." He slid it into his jacket pocket. "Maybe I'll keep it as a souvenir."

"It has to look like an accident, Leo. We don't want any heat over this." She glanced over at Liddell. "A fatal accident."

Liddell flexed his fingers cautiously, winced at the sharp tongue of flame that shot to his shoulders. The muscles in his back and legs screamed with pain, brought fresh beads of perspiration to his forehead and upper lip. Disregarding the pain, he continued to flex his fingers, managed to work some feeling into them.

"You're sure he's light?" Leo ran his hands over Liddell's pockets expertly, came up with the switchblade knife he had taken away from Angelo's stooge, Marty. The apelike man flicked open the blade, whistled softly. "A real edge. Guy could do a lot of damage with an edge like this," he remonstrated with the columnist. "You ought to be more careful, Laura."

"I got his gún, didn't I? How should I know he'd be carrying a knife as well?" She rolled her eyes to Liddell. "I guess we won't be seeing any more of each other, Liddell. It's like I told you at Johnson's party. If you behave and work with Laura, you can work this town." She shrugged. "You had other ideas." She laid her gun down on the desk, set about changing the cigarette in her holder.

For a moment, Sullivan's eyes left Liddell. He figured the chances of reaching the gun on the desk, forced his tortured muscles into a leap at it. The columnist was taken by surprise, yelled a warning to Sullivan.

He straightened up, saw what was happening. Almost as a reflex he reversed the knife in his hand, whipped it at Liddell. The private detective could hear it whiz as it went past his head. Some place there was a muffled gasp.

Liddell had no chance to find out what was happening. His fingers closed on Laura's gun as Sullivan went for his pocket, tried to pull the .45 loose. Liddell's fingers tightened around the trigger. The little automatic spat viciously. Sullivan fielded all three shots with his midsection. There was a surprised look on his face as he laced his fingers across his belly in a futile attempt to stem the red tide that was already seeping through his fingers.

His knees sagged, his eyes glazed. He pitched forward, hit the floor face first and didn't move.

Painfully, slowly, Liddell swung around to face the woman who stood behind him.

The columnists lips were pulled away from her teeth in a ghastly caricature of a grin. The handle of the knife protruded from her abdomen like some obscene horn. She had wrapped both hands around the handle, trying to tug it free. She swayed for a moment, toppled to the ground.

She was dead by the time Liddell reached her.

He walked back to the hidden file, emptied it of its folders. Then he slid the panel back into place. He started painfully for the door, stopped to glance back at the tableau.

Then, as if by afterthought, he walked back, placed the gun that had killed Sullivan alongside the dead columnist's hand. He slid a sheet of paper into the typewriter, started to type slowly, painfully. After a moment, with a grunt, he straightened up, read what he had written:

"The column has just learned that Edward Match, who has built his talent agency with amazing speed in this town, has a long and unsavory criminal record in the East. He has threatened to—"

He broke off, grinned. Then, sticking the folders under his arm, he stepped across the outstretched form of Leo Sullivan, and headed for the special elevator and the car that was waiting by the basement door.

Dead Drunk

The blonde stood at the picture window, stared down at the silver ribbon that was the East River ten stories below. The occasional hoot of a tug or the clank of a barge barely penetrated into the room.

She had been poured into a tight-fitting sheath that hinted at the sleekness of her thighs, the roundness of her hips, and gave up any pretense of disguising the cantilever construction of her façade.

The man was sprawled in an easy chair, a half-filled glass in his hand, a cigarette hung from the corner of his mouth. He was eying the snugness of her skirt around her hips with appreciation. When she turned to face him, the effect from the flip side was equally interesting.

She appeared to have made a decision. "All right, Mr. Davis—"

The man swirled the liquor around the sides of his glass. "Tim," he told her. "Mr. Davis sounds so formal."

A brief flash of annoyance clouded the slanted green eyes; the full lips narrowed into a thin slash. "Let's keep this on a business basis, shall we?" She walked over to the portable bar against the wall, picked up a glass, spilled some liquor into it and added ice. "You say you've been hired by my husband to get him the evidence he needs for a divorce." She looked over to where he sat. "So?"

Tim Davis took the cigarette from between his lips, grinned at her. "Baby, baby. You sure didn't try to do much covering up." He leaned over, crushed the cigarette out in an ash tray. "You left a trail a mile wide." He tapped his breast pocket. "I've got stuff here that would get him that decree in any court in the country." He licked at his slack lips. "Real good stuff."

The blonde took a deep swallow from her glass. "How much?"

The man in the chair shrugged. "Suppose you do buy this stuff back, Lorna—"

"Mrs. Kyler," the woman said coldly.

Davis considered, shrugged again. "Like the guy says. What's in a name? Mrs. Kyler today"—he tapped his breast pocket suggestively—"no Mrs. Kyler tomorrow. You know?"

The blonde drained her glass, set it down, walked back to the window, her full hips working smoothly against the fabric of her skirt. She stood with her back to him. "If you didn't come here to sell the information, what do you want?"

The private detective clinked the ice in his glass against the sides. "Like I was saying, Lorna. It wouldn't do any good to buy this stuff back. There's lots more around where this came from. You buy me off, there's a hundred other cops your husband could buy to get him what he wants."

"So you took the trouble to come up here to tell me how hopeless my position is. How nice of you." Lorna Kyler swung around. "If that's all—"

"Who said it was hopeless?" The man in the chair reached up, scratched at his pate where the hairline had receded. "I thought maybe you and me, we'd have a talk. I've got some ideas."

A frown ridged the blonde's forehead. "You just said—"

"I just said there's no use trying to buy up all the evidence you left behind." He pursed his lips, dropped his eyes to his half-filled glass. "As long as he's alive, you've got troubles." He rolled his eyes up from the glass to the woman's face. "Big troubles."

The blonde's shoulders drooped slightly. "You have a suggestion?"

"Accidents have been known to happen."

Lorna Kyler stared at the man in the chair for a moment, walked over, sat on the couch facing him. "You're presuming an awful lot to come here and make statements like that. Suppose I should go to the police? Or even to my husband?"

The man in the chair grinned, shook his head. "You'd be crazy to. In the first place, they wouldn't believe you. I'm a licensed private investigator doing a job for your husband. Naturally you'd try to discredit me. And when they saw what I'd managed to dig up on you"—he grinned again, shook his head—"you wouldn't stand a chance."

Lorna caught her full lower lip between her teeth, worried it. The slanted green eyes studied the face of the man in the chair opposite her. She realized she was taking a big chance if the man had been sent by her husband; on the other hand, her husband had no need for such traps. The detective was right—she had left a wide-open trail, overly confident that she could always twist Abner Kyler around her finger.

"Why should you do this?" she asked finally.

Tim Davis took a deep swallow from his glass. "Money." He leaned back, rubbed the heel of his hand along his chin. "Either way, I can't lose. You don't buy the idea, I take what I've got to the old man. You buy it, I make triple my fee."

"I see." The blonde got up out of her chair, made another trip to the window. "How much is that fee?"

The detective considered. "You get the whole package for a hundred thousand."

The woman at the window whirled. "You must be crazy. A hundred thousand! Why—"

"There'll still be plenty left. A lot more than if I turn over what I've found." He managed to look sad. "That way we're both out."

Lorna started to argue, then shrugged. "I'd be the first one they'd suspect." She shook her head. "It wouldn't work."

"Why don't you leave that to me?" Davis told her.

"You'd be out of town when it happened. There'd be no way they could tie you to it." He tilted the glass to his lips, drained it. "I'm not exactly an amateur."

The blonde couldn't repress a slight shudder, rubbed the backs of her arms with the palms of her hands. "How would it happen?"

Tim Davis leaned over, deposited the empty glass on the edge of the coffee table. "Leave that up to me, too. The less you know about it, the less you're likely to spill if they do start questioning you." He consulted his watch. "Is there some place you can go for let's say a week?"

The blonde bobbed her head. "I have friends up on the Cape." She licked at her lips. "Would it take that long? I mean . . . "

The man in the chair pulled himself to his feet. "Don't worry about when it's going to happen. That way you'll be all the more surprised when they send for you." He made an ineffectual attempt to smooth some of the creases out of his pants. "I'll be in touch in about ten days." He walked to the door, stopped with his hand on the knob, turned back. "If you have any idea of reneging on the price, forget it. The money wouldn't do you any good in a shroud." He pasted a grin on his lips that failed to make his eyes, pulled the door open and closed it after him.

Lorna Kyler stood looking at the door for a moment, then ran to it. She reached for the knob, hesitated, then dropped her hand. She turned, walked back to the portable bar, poured herself a stiff drink.

In the hallway, Tim Davis waited for two minutes, then grinned his self-satisfaction. He knew he had her figured right from the minute he started digging into her background. But even some of these case-hardened babes backed away from murder. He was glad she didn't.

Johnny Liddell walked down the corridor to the double glass door at the far end of the hall bearing the inscription *Seaway Insurance Corp.* He pushed through into the anteroom, walked up to the girl at the desk in the enclosed area.

"Lee Devon."

The girl behind the desk stopped pecking at the typewriter keys and turned a pair of incurious eyes on him. "May I have your name?"

"Johnny Liddell."

"Mr. Devon's expecting you." She got up from her chair, waited until Liddell had pushed through the gate, turned and headed for an office diagonally across from her desk. "Will you walk this way, please?"

Liddell watched for a moment, shook his head sadly. "Sorry, honey. Wish I could."

The girl gave no sign that she'd heard, held the door open for him. He had an impression of full breasts and firm thighs as he squeezed past her into the room.

Lee Devon looked as if he had been jammed into the armchair behind the desk. He was fat and soft-looking, and was swabbing his forehead with a balled handkerchief as Liddell walked in. His eyes were two bright-blue marbles that were almost lost behind the puffy pouches that buttressed them. He nodded to the girl, his jowls swinging. "I don't want any calls, Janie." When the girl had closed the door behind her, he turned to Liddell. "Sit down, Johnny. I think we've got some business for you."

Liddell pulled a chair up to the desk, dropped into it.

Devon picked up a folder from the corner of his desk, flipped it open. "You read about Abner Kyler?" He rolled his eyes upward, studied Liddell from under heavily veined lids. "Millionaire, got himself boxed out of his mind, got himself killed when his car went through a railing over the viaduct leading to the Hamptons."

Liddell reached over to the humidor on the desk, helped himself to a cigarette. He stuck it in the corner of his mouth. "I read something about it," he said. He scratched a match, touched it to the cigarette. "You don't think that's how it happened. That it?"

The fat man picked up a cigar, tested it between thumb and forefinger. He pursed his lips, made and broke bubbles between them. "Let's just say that I want you to find out if that is the way it happened."

"Any reason for thinking it wasn't?"

Devon bit the end off the cigar, spat it at the waste basket. He stuck it between his teeth, chewed on it. "Nothing I can put my finger on. Just a feeling." He held the unlit cigar in the center of his mouth, seemed to be selecting his words. "You fly a desk like this for twenty years, you get a feeling every so often." He squirmed uncomfortably in his chair. "I'm not as active as I used to be, so I figured maybe you'd like to check this one out for me."

Liddell nodded. "What've you got?"

The man behind the desk shoved the folder toward him. Liddell dumped the contents on the desk, skimmed through a flimsy on the police report, glanced at the findings of the coroner.

"Alcohol concentration point three in his blood?" Liddell whistled. "This boy didn't do things halfway."

The fat man bobbed his head, starting the jowls swinging. "According to the A.M.A., a concentration of point one five would mean he'd had twelve ounces of hundred-proof stuff. A point three concentration would mean twenty-four ounces."

Liddell dropped his eyes back to the coroner's report, then picked up a glossy showing a smashed car lying on its top, the tangled legs of a body visible inside it. A second picture showed the dead man after he had been removed from the car, his head lopsided, his eyes staring blankly upward.

Liddell flipped the glossies back on the desk, turned to the coroner's report, checked through it, grunted. "Compound fracture of the right frontal." He looked across the desk at Devon. "You'd think the wheel would be enough to keep him from cracking his head against the windshield, wouldn't you? A broken neck, or the top of his head crushed in, sure. But the front of his head caved in ..." He shook his head.

"Anything could happen in a freak accident like that. When it crashed through the barrier, the car did a flip, landed on its roof twenty feet below." Devon chewed on the unlit cigar, half-veiled his eyes with the heavily veined lids. "Thing that bothers me is that there was still plenty of alcohol in his stomach." He pulled the cigar from between his teeth, touched his tongue to a loose strand of tobacco, pasted the cigar back into place. "But it was after four o'clock and there wasn't a bar open within fifty miles. No sign of a bottle in the car or anyplace near it."

Johnny Liddell leaned back, nodded thoughtfully. "I read you real clear. Who benefits?"

The fat man screwed his features into a grimace. "Dry run. His wife collects everything. We checked her out real good. She spent the four days up to the accident on the Cape with friends. No phone calls, no letters, never out of sight."

"But?"

The fat man shrugged his shoulders, spilling his jowls over the side of his collar. "This wife—she's half his age, stacked. From what I gather, she's been living it up but good for the past few years."

"Have a talk with her?"

Devon grunted, shook his head. "She has a real fancy-pants lawyer. The boys upstairs have turned hands down on anything but polite conversation unless we got something concrete. And this we don't have."

Liddell got up from his chair, walked over to where a water cooler was humming softly to itself, drew a paper cup full of water. "You say she was young and pretty. Maybe the old man knew about her cutting up and figured that was a small price for rent on the chassis?"

The fat man pulled the cigar from between his teeth, stared at the soggy end, bounced it in the waste basket. "He wasn't. He wanted out. At least, he had a later model he wanted to trade her in on. And from the little we've been able to dig, he wouldn't have had much trouble doing it. If he hadn't gone and got himself dead."

"And the model?"

"Gita Ravell, a little redhead who acted as his secretary. She claimed she saw him earlier that night, that he left her about one and that at that point he hadn't had a drink. A couple of hours later, about fifty miles away, he shows up reeking of alcohol and dead." He sighed lugubriously. "And that's all she did have. Suspicion. I let Legal talk to her and they ruled it out. But she still insists he wasn't much of a drinker. Definitely not in that point-three-concentration league. She never saw him take more than two Scotches, she insists." He raised his hands, palms out. "Not much to give you, but that's the story. Think you can do anything with it?"

Liddell scowled. "Like you say, it's not much. Where do I find this Gita Ravell?"

"Kyler had an office in the Graybar Building." He leaned forward, pulled a desk calendar toward him, flipped back a few pages. "She has a pad in the Village. Fifty-one Perry." He sank back with a sigh. "I think you're wasting your time talking to her. Our boys pumped her for everything she has. Nothing." He stared down at his hands clasped across his midsection, dimples where the knuckles should have been. "Our only hope is to break down the wife." He rolled his eyes upward, shook his head. "And that's not going to be easy."

The directory listed Mrs. Abner Kyler's address as the Cathedral Arms on East End Avenue. It turned out to be an oppressively modern pile of bricks and plate glass towering over the East River at 89th Street.

Johnny Liddell dropped the cab at the curb, headed across the lobby to where a rheumy-eyed old man in a dark jacket stood guard at the desk.

"Mrs. Kyler. Mrs. Abner Kyler," Liddell told him.

The clerk deigned to consider it, shook his head judiciously. "Mrs. Kyler isn't receiving. There's been a loss, you know."

"Suppose you ask her. Tell her I'm a private detective and I've been doing some work for her husband. I thought she might be interested in what I discovered for him."

The clerk *tsk-tsk*ed his annoyance, made a production of picking up the desk phone. He murmured into it, waited, then replaced it on its hook. "Mrs. Kyler will see you," he told Liddell with no show of enthusiasm. "She's in Suite Ten F." He wrinkled his nose, dabbed a handkerchief at his rheumy eyes, followed Liddell's progress toward the elevator bank with disapproval.

The elevator whooshed gently to a stop at the tenth floor, the door sighed open. Suite 10F was at the end of the corridor, facing out over the East River.

The woman who opened the door in response to Johnny Liddell's knock was tall, blond. He ran his eyes appraisingly from the top of her blond head to her sandaled feet with appropriate stops on the way.

"Mrs. Abner Kyler? My name's Johnny Liddell. I'm a private detective."

The woman stepped aside, permitted him to enter the large living room, closed the door behind him. In the light of the room, he could see that she was a little older than her silhouette would indicate, but still comfortably on the right side of thirty-five.

"All right, mister," she snapped. "Now suppose you tell me what this is all about." The slanted green eyes snapped angrily, the full lips were drawn into a thin red line.

"It's just like the lilac-scented character on the desk told you—"

"You were working for my husband and wanted to tell me what you'd found out," she mimicked. "You're a liar. Look, mister. I don't have to put up with this. Either you level with me right now, or I call the police. What are you doing here?"

Liddell scratched at the side of his jaw. "Your husband wanted a divorce, lady, and—"

"You've got things a little mixed up, haven't you? I'm the one who wanted the divorce. And if he'd lived a few weeks more, I would have got it."

Liddell managed to look confused. "Maybe you didn't know it, but your husband did a complete check of your background."

The blonde sneered at him. "My husband knew what I was when I married him; he went into it with his eyes wide open. I never tried to hide from him the fact that I hated being married to an old man and that I wanted out. He refused to give me a divorce, even flaunted that redheaded floozy he was keeping in my face. Just a few more weeks . . ." She brushed past Liddell, picked up a cigarette from a pack on the coffee table, tapped it against her thumb-nail. "Who really sent you? The Ravell woman?"

Liddell scratched at his head, found a match, lit the blonde's cigarette. "Actually I'm checking out a report that your husband wasn't much of a drinker, that he never would normally have been as boxed out as he was that night."

Lorna Kyler filled her lungs with a deep drag, let the smoke dribble from between parted lips. She turned her back on him, walked to the window. When she turned back, some of the anger seemed to have drained from her face. "Who'd know more of a man's vices? His wife—or some young floozy he had big eyes for?" She indicated the filled bar at the side of the room. "It was one of Abner's worst failings. There were days on end when he'd just lie here and empty bottle after bottle."

Liddell held his hands up. "That's what I wanted to know. I'm sorry if I upset you. I was just trying to earn a fee."

The blonde studied him, seemed to be seeing him for the first time. "I'm sorry, too. It's just that—well, I don't like the insinuations. I don't like the way the insurance company is trying to twist this thing around." She dropped her voice. "But that's no reason for me to take it out on you." She indicated the bar. "Would you like a drink? I could use a Scotch." She walked over and perched on the arm of a chair.

Liddell walked over to the bar, dropped ice into two glasses, spilled some Scotch over them. He brought one back to the blonde.

She smiled up at him. "I'm not always this inhospitable." She brought the glass to her lips with a shaking hand, spilled most of it down the front of her gown. "Damn!" she exclaimed. She swabbed at the wet portion with a hopelessly inadequate wisp of linen, stood up. "Pardon me while I get into something dry." She headed for the bedroom.

Johnny Liddell took his drink, wandered to the picture window, stared down at the river below. The blonde had made no attempt to hide the unsavory past Lee Devon had indicated, but what the insurance man apparently didn't take into consideration was the woman's contention that it was she, not Abner Kyler, who wanted the divorce. He sighed, took a deep swallow from the glass. If she could make that stand up, it would be understandable that Kyler might have got himself boxed out, especially in view of her statement that he was a secret drinker. It could even be suicide, if she could project the picture of an old man who felt things closing in on him. Liddell swore under his breath. Either way, Lorna Kyler wasn't the type to do too much leaning on.

He had finished his drink and was building a refill when the door to the bedroom opened and the blonde reappeared. She had changed into a loose, nile-green dressing gown.

"Sorry to be so long." She smiled at him. "I promise not to be so clumsy if you'll make me a new one." She walked to the couch, dropped down onto it, watched him make a second drink. "Why can't we be friendly instead of tossing implied threats at each other?"

"I'd prefer it that way," Liddell conceded. He brought her drink over to the couch, dropped down alongside her. "Like I said, I'm only earning a fee."

The woman took a deep swallow from the glass, nodded. "I'll tell you the whole story." She leaned forward, set her glass on the coffee table, turned the full power of the slanted eyes on him. "That is, if you're sure you won't be bored."

He wasn't.

It was growing dark when Johnny Liddell walked out of the Cathedral Arms and waved down a cruising cab. He gave the cabby the address of the redheaded secretary, leaned back against the cushions, speculated on what Lorna Kyler had been trying to tell him in her rambling story of a small-town cigarette girl who'd married an elderly millionaire. He finally gave up.

Fifty-one Perry Street was a brownstone building nestling anonymously in a row of identical brownstones. Liddell climbed four steps from the sidewalk level, pushed his way through the vestibule door. A highly polished brass letter box supplied the information that Gita Ravell occupied street floor rear. He followed the dimly lit hallway to the rear apartment, knocked.

When there was no response to his second knock, he tried the knob. It turned easily in his hand. He pushed the door open and stepped into the small vestibule. The room beyond was in darkness accentuated by drawn shades.

As he closed the hallway door behind him, he was aware of an oddly familiar smell pervading the room —a sickly smell that made his nostrils twitch, the hair on the back of his neck rise.

He fumbled for the light switch, spilled light into the room beyond.

Gita Ravell sat in a chair facing the doorway. Her hair was a thick coppery pile on the top of her head; her eyes were half closed, her lips parted as though she were on the verge of saying something.

The ugly, gaping wound in her throat made it improbable that she would ever finish what she had started to say.

Johnny Liddell stared at her, swore under his breath. He walked over to the chair, laid his hand against her cheek. The skin was beginning to cool. He reached down, caught her sleeve, lifted her arm. Clutched clumsily in her fist was a long-bladed knife, its edge red-tinged.

Liddell straightened up, looked around the apartment. There was no sign of a struggle, no evidence to support his conviction that the girl's fingers had been wrapped around the handle after her throat had been slashed. He bent over the body again, examined the gaping wound. It was a clean slash, no sign of the hesitation marks, the telltale little scratches that invariably precede the lethal cut in a suicide. It satisfied him that the girl had been murdered, but the district attorney might require more proof.

Liddell stared at the face of the girl, once undoubtedly pretty, now caricatured by death. He wondered why it would be necessary to murder her, tried to imagine what she could have known that made her dangerous. In his mind's eye, he reviewed everything he knew about the case. Gita Ravell had insisted Kyler was murdered, but she had nothing to prove her contention. Or did she have something she wasn't aware of? Something the killer was afraid she'd remember or find?

Suddenly, as he studied the face of the dead girl, things began to fall into place. He again checked the warmth of the dead girl's cheek, made a fast estimate of the time of death. It was a hunch that would require checking in the morning—but for the first time, things were beginning to make sense.

It was after midnight when Tim Davis stalked into the lobby of the Cathedral Arms. He ignored the night man behind the desk, headed for the elevator bank, pushed the button for the tenth floor.

Lorna Kyler opened the door in response to his knock, drew in her breath sharply when she recognized the private detective. "What are you doing here?"

"Let me in. Or do you want me to discuss our business from out here?"

The door swung open. Tim Davis pushed through, closed it behind him.

"You should know better than to come here at this hour," the blonde stormed at him. "You gone crazy?"

"No. But maybe you have. If you're trying to pull something." He pulled an edition of the *News* from his pocket, shoved it at her.

She stared at him, dropped her eyes to the front page of the tab, walked into the living room, held it under a lamp. After a moment, she looked up, wide-eyed. "Gita Ravell was murdered last night. You?"

"That's not the point. She was discovered by Johnny Liddell. The same Johnny Liddell you were supposed to be keeping here until I had a talk with Ravell. A few minutes earlier and he might have walked in on me." He caught the blonde's arm, squeezed it cruelly. "If I thought you tried—"

Lorna Kyler shook her head. "I didn't. I kept him here as long as I could. I thought you were only going to reason with her."

"She knew too much. The canceled checks came back today. One of them was made out to me. Signed by Kyler." He dug his hand into his pocket, brought out a check. "It could blow hell out of our story."

The color drained from the blonde's face, leaving her make-up as garish blobs on the pallor. "And now?"

Tim Davis tore the check into pieces, dropped them into an ash tray, touched a match to them. "I fixed it to look like she did the Dutch." He looked up from the ash tray. "They'll figure she was so upset about the old man dying, she cut her own throat." He grinned crookedly. "But I guess this changes our deal."

"I should have known. I suppose you want more money." The woman's lips were twisted with contempt. "Your kind always does."

"Is that a nice thing to say to your prospective husband?"

Lorna stared for a moment. "Prospective husband? Now I know you're crazy. If you think I—"

Davis grinned crookedly. "No. I don't think you want to sit in the electric chair. That's why you're going to marry me. A wife can't testify against a husband, you know." The grin became strained. "But it's a two-way street. A husband can't testify against a wife, either."

"Testify about what? All I did was keep Liddell here while you went to talk to the girl. I didn't know you were going to kill her."

"I know that, baby. And so do you. But if they ever started putting the heat on me at headquarters, who knows what I'd be likely to say. You know?"

"That's blackmail."

"Insurance, baby. Electric-chair insurance. And the premium isn't very high."

"Just half of everything I've got."

"Look what you get in return. You get to keep on living."

The blonde shook her head from side to side. "It won't work, I tell you. They'd smell a rat in a minute if I were to marry you so soon after Abner—"

"Nobody has to know. We don't announce it for a year or so unless they get lucky and stumble on something." A hard note crept into his voice. "Don't forget it's for your good as well as mine. If I get to sit in that chair, you'll be sitting in my lap."

The blonde stared at him with stricken eyes. "There's no other way?"

"That's not very flattering, baby. Good thing I'm not sensitive." Davis grinned at her. The grin got broader as she swung away from him, headed for the bar and poured herself a stiff slug of Scotch. She swallowed it in one gulp, coughed as it burned her throat. "When do we do it? Get married, I mean?" she asked without turning around.

Davis shrugged. "The sooner the better. We can drive out tonight, get down to Baltimore, get it over with and be back before morning."

Lorna poured herself another drink, swallowed it slowly. She set the glass down, bobbed her head jerkily. "Okay. I'll get dressed. I won't be long."

Davis nodded. "Sure, baby. Only leave the door open. Just so I know you're not making any phone calls. Like the one you made to me while Liddell was here. The one where you told me to take care of the redhead."

Lorna whirled on him, started to retort, shrugged her shoulders. She headed for the bedroom, left the door open.

Davis grinned as she disappeared into the other room, licked his lips in anticipation. He poured himself two fingers of liquor, sipped it contentedly. He was almost finished with his drink when the girl reappeared in the doorway. He frowned his displeasure when he noticed she hadn't begun to change.

"I told you as soon as possible, baby." The hard note was back in his voice. He saw the .38 in her hand for the first time, gasped as she brought it into firing position. "You crazy? I warned you—"

"Sure. You warned me—husbands can't testify against their wives. But neither can dead men."

Davis dropped his glass, his hand streaked for his lapel. The gun in the girl's hand bucked, spat yellow flame. The detective's body staggered backward as the slug hit him. He struggled to free his gun from its holster, fielded two more slugs in the midsection. He laced his hands across his body in a futile effort to stem the flow of red that was already beginning to seep through his fingers. His knees buckled under him, he hit the floor face first, didn't move.

Lorna Kyler moved swiftly. She scooped up the glass Davis had been using, quickly dried it and replaced it on the bar. Then she ran to the hall door, pulled it open, started screaming.

Inspector Herlehy of Homicide stood at the picture window, stared down at the river below. Behind him, the men from the medical examiner's office were lifting Tim Davis's body onto a stretcher. They covered him with a blanket, strapped him on. One of the men approached the inspector, held out a form to be initialed.

Herlehy looked up at the knock on the door, scowled when he recognized the newcomer as Johnny Liddell. He initialed the form, gave it back to the man from the mortuary section.

"What are you doing here, Johnny?" he wanted to know.

"Representing Seaway Insurance, Inspector." Liddell nodded to the shrouded body on the stretcher. "My company has an interest in this character. When word came through that he got himself dead, they asked me to drop by."

"What kind of interest?"

Liddell shrugged. "A big client, Abner Kyler, was supposedly killed in an automobile accident. This character had been doing a tail job on Abner. Supposed to have been keeping an eye on the old man and his secretary."

Herlehy suddenly looked as though he had a sour taste in his mouth. "The one who cut her throat." He nodded toward the dead man. "Davis tried to blackmail her and she couldn't face it. So we're sending him down to keep her company."

Liddell pursed his lips. "Where'd you get all this?"

"Mrs. Kyler. Davis came here after he left the secretary. He read about the secretary doing the Dutch in the early edition of the tabs, and he saw a chance to make some real money by selling the whole story to a

scandal magazine. He wanted money from Mrs. Kyler
to keep quiet about the whole mess." He shrugged.
"She didn't want the scandal so she started to argue
with him. When he started to push her around, she
tried to call the police. In the struggle, she killed him."

Liddell considered it, nodded. "Sounds like it could
happen."

"The night clerk saw the guy come in. He wasn't
here much more than fifteen minutes when the shooting and screaming started." Herlehy pushed his hat to
the back of his head. "Want to talk to Mrs. Kyler?"

Liddell nodded.

The inspector led the way to the bedroom door,
knocked. There was a muffled invitation to enter. He
turned the knob, pushed the door open.

The room beyond was a large bedroom with a small
balcony that overlooked the river. The blonde was
sprawled out on the bed, a handkerchief pressed
against her mouth. She sat up when she saw Liddell,
then looked from him to the inspector and back.

"Mr. Liddell! You heard?"

Liddell nodded. "What happened?"

"He tried to blackmail me. When I refused, he beat
me. He threatened to kill me. I managed to get the
gun—"

"You did real good, chickie, but it was a waste of
time." He turned to Herlehy. "On my advice, Seaway
will refuse to pay the claim on Abner Kyler." He
looked back to the woman on the bed. "We're convinced it was no accident."

Lorna Kyler jumped to her feet. "What are you
saying?"

"We're saying that Abner Kyler was killed because
you wanted his money and you knew you wouldn't get
a cent if he got his evidence against you into a divorce
court. So you made a deal with Davis to kill him."

"You crazy?" the girl gasped. "I hired Davis to get
evidence of his carrying on with the Ravell woman."

"You can stop lying, chickie. Davis was working

for your husband. That's why Davis was able to get him."

Herlehy scowled. "You can prove some of this, I hope?"

Liddell turned to the Inspector. "That's why the secretary had to be killed. The canceled checks came back today, and when she saw the retainer check made out to Tim Davis, she put two and two together."

"You can't prove that," the blonde snapped. "There is no such check."

"Don't count on it, chickie. Even if Tim Davis did destroy the check itself, the bank makes photostats of all checks paid out."

Herlehy watched the play of emotion on the girl's face. "Even so, why should she kill Davis?"

"It was getting too hot. Maybe he raised the ante? With you thrown in for a bonus?" The blonde stared at him, started to back away. "You kept me here while he went to scare the redhead," Liddell continued. "That bit of spilling the liquor on the dress was pretty transparent. But I couldn't figure out why. When I found the redhead dead, I knew."

The girl started to shake uncontrollably. "You're wrong," she muttered. "All wrong."

Liddell shook his head. "We haven't got all the pieces yet, chickie. But now that we know where to look, it won't take long."

The blonde continued to stare at him for a moment, then with a scream, she turned and ran for the balcony. Liddell looked away, heard the inspector swear as he started after her. When Liddell looked up, the balcony was empty. The inspector was leaning over the edge, looking down.

From somewhere below there was the sound of a soul in agony, then with breath-taking suddenness, there was quiet.

Dead Reckoning

Johnny Liddell was only listening to Russo with half an ear.

The redhead speared to the center of the floor by the spotlight was leaning against the piano. She looked as though she had been poured into the iridescent green gown that seemed to be pasted to her body. Her hair was molten copper, hung down over her shoulders, her skin gleamed a milky white.

When she straightened up to take a bow at the end of the number, her body seemed to flow—as though it was boneless. Every movement was sensuous, suggestive. As she bowed her head to the thunder of applause that rolled toward her from the dimly lit tables, her neckline dipped alarmingly.

The man across the table from Liddell scowled irritably as his eyes followed the magnet to Liddell's attention. Tony Russo wasn't used to people listening to him with half an ear. Not even if he was asking them to do him a favor.

"Look, Liddell. You dig the redhead that much, I'll see you meet her. But right now I want to know. You handle my case for me or not?"

Liddell reluctantly tore his eyes from the redhead, brought them into focus on the man across the table.

"You know I don't hire out my gun, Tony."

Russo groaned his frustration. "Who the hell asks you to hire out your gun? I want to make a hit, I got plenty of boys of my own."

"So why don't you have one of your boys handle it?"

"Because they don't have the one thing I'm trying to hire. Brains."

The redhead had started to sing again. She was leaning against the piano. Her voice was husky, the kind that plays along the spinal column like a xylophone. The lyrics were blue, but she managed to retain an expression of untroubled innocence despite the bursts of laughter some of the lines drew.

Johnny Liddell fought a losing battle to keep his attention on what Tony Russo was telling him, let his eyes wander back onto the floor.

"All right, all right. You can't keep your eyes off the broad. You want to meet me in my office after the show's over?"

Liddell nodded. "You said something about meeting her?"

Russo snorted disgustedly, got to his feet. "I'll have her up there, too." He turned, felt his way through the tables in the darkened room toward the entrance.

When the redhead had finished her number, she smiled at the cascade of applause, shook her head to demands for an encore. She threw kisses at the occupants of the ringside tables, headed for the rhinestoned entrance to the back-stage area. She stood for a moment in the spotlight, then the floor went dark. When the lights came up, the floor was empty.

Liddell let his breath out in a soundless whistle, leaned back and fitted a cigarette into the corner of his mouth.

A heavy shouldered man with a head that looked like a cue ball with twisted lumps of scar tissue for eyebrows and a nose flattened against his face, walked over to where Liddell sat.

"The boss says when you're ready, I show you to the office."

Liddell looked up, grinned at the bald-headed man. "Hi, Maxie. Long time no see. Working for Russo now, huh?"

Maxie grinned. "Always did, Johnny. Doc Parker fronted as my manager. Tony did all the booking and fixing." He shrugged heavy shoulders. "I can't make it any more in the ring, so he gives me a job as his body-guard."

"Real generous of him."

"I got no beef, shamus. So I'm all punched out and maybe punched up. But I ain't kicking. I had a couple of years I lived real good. Real good. If I didn't have Russo behind me, I wouldn't even have that. I'd be driving a truck or smashing cases on the docks. You know?"

Liddell considered it, nodded. "You could look at it that way," he conceded.

"You don't pasture in no field of daisies yourself. You set yourself up as a target for any red-hot who's coming on too fast for the guy who pays your tab. No?"

The private detective took a last drag on the ciga-rette, crushed it out. "Maybe you're right." He looked around for his waiter, waved him down.

"No tab," Maxie told him. "The boss picks up the hot."

Liddell dropped a bill on the table for the waiter. "What is it, old age or a scare that's making Tony so generous?"

The bald-headed man managed to look hurt. "You got the boss all wrong, making him out like a hard guy. He's a real generous guy, Johnny."

"Sure. With everybody else's blood."

Maxie started to retort, shrugged, led the way through the tables toward the small foyer. A small corridor led to the cage of a self-service elevator. Maxie waved him in, punched the button marked *3* on the panel. The cage rocked its wheezy way upward, shuddered to a stop on the third floor and the door scraped open. A balcony ran from the elevator to a door marked *Private.*

The bald-headed man knocked three times, the door clicked open.

Tony Russo looked up from the fat panatela he was rolling between his thumb and forefinger, nodded Lid-dell to a chair across the highly polished desk from him. "Hang around outside, Maxie." He swiveled his eyes to the bald-headed man. "We don't want to be disturbed."

"Except by the redhead," Liddell amended. "Show her right in." He rolled his eyes to the man behind the desk. "Right, Tony?"

Russo growled deep in his chest, bobbed his head irritably. "Okay. But no one else." He waited until the bald-headed man had closed the door behind him. "You sure got somethin' for that broad."

Liddell grinned. "Sexiest looking babe I've seen in a long time."

Russo swung his chair around, slid back the disguised panel of a built-in bar. He grabbed a bottle, two glasses, set them down on the desk. "Sexy?" he grunted. "To her, sex is the number that comes after five and before seven." He saw the disbelief in Liddell's eyes. "Sure, she looks good for a fast fling. But with her it's not sex—it's either an audition or a request for a pay raise." He hit his chest with the side of his hand. "Ask Tony. He knows."

Liddell watched as Tony spilled a generous slug into each of the glasses. He got some ice from the small refrigerator built into the bar, filled the glass with the cubes, pushed one across the desk.

The years had made a change in Tony Russo, Liddell noticed. The lean wolfishness of the days of his climb to head of his pack was blurred by the soft overlay of fat. Fat, lusterless eyes still peered from beneath the heavily veined, thickened eyelids, but the soft, discolored pouches beneath them lessened the menace.

"You wanted help, Tony. What kind of help?"

Russo stuck the unlighted cigar between his teeth, chewed on it for a moment. "This is just between you and me, Liddell." He squinted at the private detective. "I don't want nobody having a big laugh on Tony Russo, thinking he's going soft."

"Seems to me I heard about a lot of guys who thought that way never broke fifty."

Russo shrugged. "Rumors." He grinned, some of the old wolfishness showing through. "Nobody fooled around with Tony in the old days." The smile faded. "That's why this is got to be some kind of screwball."

He pulled a key chain from his pocket, unlocked the top drawer of the desk. He reached in, brought out a packet of letters, tossed them across the desk. Liddell reached for them.

There were five letters, all in ordinary envelopes, all with Tony Russo's name printed in block letters, none of them postmarked. Liddell dumped the messages from the envelopes, glanced at each. He looked up, grinned at the man behind the desk.

"So somebody says you're due to get hit. So what's new about that? You've had a check mark next to your name before this."

Russo chewed angrily on the cold cigar. "Sure, but I knew who they were and where they were. You see those notes? You know where I find them? In my bathroom. Under my pillow. On my desk." He yanked the cigar from between his teeth, glared at the soggy end, then bounced it off the waste basket. "Places nobody can get. Nobody."

"How about the guys who work for you?" He nodded toward the closed door. "Maxie, for instance?"

"Why should he? I keep him eating." A thoughtful frown ridged Russo's forehead. His eyes sought out the closed door; he squinted. "I been pretty good to him. What'd a punchy like that do if it wasn't for me keeping him in bread?"

"It doesn't have to be Maxie." Liddell reached over, wrapped his fingers around the damp glass, swirled the liquor over the ice. "Maybe one of the other boys. No guy likes to stay number two boy all his life. Maybe with you out of the way—"

Russo considered, shook his head. "If I just find the notes here, okay. They maybe sneak in here and leave them. But not in my pad. No one gets into my bedroom, my john—"

There was a discreet knock on the door; it opened. The hairless dome of Maxie popped in. "The redhead, Boss."

Russo's eyes rolled from Maxie to Liddell. They were narrowed in speculation. "Yeah, the redhead." He nodded slowly. "Send her in."

Maxie's head disappeared, the doorway was filled with Woman. She had exchanged the green dress for a more practical model. Her coppery hair spilled down over her shoulders in a metallic wave. The swelling bosom showed over the top of the low-cut dress; a small waist hinted at the full hips, long shapely legs concealed by the fullness of her skirt.

As she walked in, she turned the full power of slanted, green eyes on Liddell. They seemed to approve of what they saw. She didn't waste a glance on the man behind the desk.

"Okay, Liddell, you wanted to meet her. This is Chinchilla Conover. He's Johnny Liddell, a private eye, Chilly."

"That a name or a description?" Liddell asked.

"Depends on who's using it." The slanted eyes sought out Russo. "Tony says it's a description. You mightn't."

Russo's face darkened. "I forgot to tell you, Liddell. She don't only sing. She makes with the funny remarks, too." He got up from behind the desk, walked around. He made a production out of scooping up the letters and envelopes, tapped his fingernail against them. "I think you told me what I wanted to know, Liddell. Send me a bill." His eyes never left the redhead's face.

She glanced briefly at the letters, then admired the finish on her long, carefully shellacked nails. "Fan mail, Tony?"

Russo's hand shot out, the sound when it connected with the side of the girl's face sounded like a shot. It knocked her sideways. He back-handed her face into position.

Liddell moved fast. He caught Russo by the front of

his jacket, pushed him across the room. The café owner's legs tangled with a low coffee table, he spilled to the floor in its wreckage.

"I don't like guys who work out on girls, Russo. You ought to remember that from the old days."

Russo's face was white as he struggled to disentangle his legs from the shattered table. "Maxie," he roared.

The door popped open, the cue-ball head of the ex-pug appeared in the opening. His eyes hopscotched from Liddell to Russo and back.

"Take him," Russo growled. "Take him good."

"Tony, wait a minute—" Chilly was massaging the side of her face, still stained with red.

"You stay out of this, you! Nobody pushes Tony Russo around." He turned back to Maxie. "What are you waiting for? I told you to take him."

Maxie reached up, took out his upper plate, dropped it into his pocket. Then, hunching his shoulders so that his head was almost lost between them, he started shuffling toward Liddell. As he slouched forward he licked at his lips with anticipation.

"Take him good, Maxie," Russo ordered.

Liddell didn't take his eyes off the bodyguard. He kept watching, waiting for an opening.

Maxie moved in with a speed surprising in a man of his size. He shot a hard right at Johnny's face. Liddell swayed out of its path, brought his left up into the bald-headed man's midsection. Maxie roared like a stung bear, continued to bore in. He caught Liddell on the side of the head with a ham-sized fist that started the lights flashing and bells ringing in Johnny's head. The big paw landed again and Liddell felt the floor slope upward and hit him in the face.

"Stamp him!" Russo ordered.

As Maxie raised his foot, the redhead threw herself at him, her fingers clenched, the nails going for the big man's face. He caught her by the wrists, sent her sprawling across the floor. She lay here, legs askew, dress twisted over her thighs. Maxie licked at his lips, stared at her for a moment.

A moment was all Liddell needed. He forced air into his lungs, shook his head to dispel the fog. As the big man turned his attention back to the man sprawled in front of him, Liddell's head cleared.

"Nothing personal, shamus." Maxie brought his foot up, aimed the heavy heel at the detective's head and kicked. Liddell rolled over, caught the foot and twisted. Maxie hit the floor with a thump that rattled the glasses on the desk.

Liddell struggled to his feet, watched the snarling, cursing bald-headed man pulling himself up. He waited grimly for Maxie to resume the assault.

The bald-headed man threw caution to the winds, rushed him. Liddell side-stepped, planted his right to the elbow in Maxie's midsection. As the bodyguard toppled over, Liddell brought up his knee, caught him in the face. There was a crunching sound as the man's nose broke again. Liddell chopped down at the exposed back of the other man's neck in a vicious rabbit punch. Maxie hit the floor, face first, didn't move.

Liddell looked up from the fallen man to Russo, who backed away until the wall was at his back. Johnny sneered at him, walked over to the girl, helped her to her feet.

She eyed him with new interest.

"You're quite a man, Liddell. I never saw anybody stand up to Maxie before and walk away from it."

"It was nothing. I was flea-weight champ at P.S. 64 in 1929." He grinned at her. "Besides, I had you on my side. If you hadn't given me a breather by trying to carve your initials on his kisser, he might have done a pretty good job of changing my face around." From the corner of his eye, he saw Russo skirt the desk, head for a button on the base of the phone. He reached past the girl, caught Russo by the shirt front, pulled him up on his toes.

Russo's eyes were white-rimmed with fear. "Don't muscle me, Liddell. You're not scaring me—"

Chilly grinned. "You could fool me. I can't tell whether it's castanets or your teeth. Whatever it is, it's making pretty music."

"I'm not forgetting you, either," Russo told her. "I'll get you for this and for—"

Liddell's hand cracked across his mouth, knocked Russo's head back. A thin trickle of blood ran from the corner of the café owner's mouth.

"I'm leaving you teeth, Tony, just so I'll have something to work on if I have to come back." He reached under his jacket, brought out his .45, held it under Russo's nose. "If I do have to come back, I'm using this to leave you as toothless as the day you were born. You leave her alone. You dig?"

Russo's eyes seemed to be hypnotized by the yawning muzzle of the .45. He could only nod his head wordlessly. Liddell pushed him, he collapsed into a bundle of arms and legs in the big armchair.

Liddell turned to the girl. "Whose idea was the notes?"

The slanted eyes widened, the redhead shook her head. "I don't know what you mean?"

"You left a trail like a bulldozer through the Everglades, baby. You signed them by leaving them where nobody else could have been."

Chilly started to deny it, shrugged. "I just wanted to see him squirm. You should have been here, Liddell. It was the only thing that made it possible for me to stay in the same room with him. To watch him squirming and sweating—"

"You're lying," Russo roared. "Nobody scares Tony Russo."

The redhead laughed at him. "He wouldn't go out. Somebody had to taste his meals. He became practically a hermit. You weren't scared. Not much!"

"You know you wouldn't have gotten away with it. The cops would have tumbled just the way I did—"

"I wasn't going to kill him. I was just going to watch him shake himself to pieces. Every day he got worse.

I wanted revenge. I was getting it. Just watching him
fall apart. Watching his boys know it and him knowing
they knew he'd gone soft. It was worth it. Every bit of
it."

"You wanted revenge. Revenge for what?"

"My real name is Bauer. Lynn Bauer. That mean
anything to you?"

Russo's eyes widened. "Bauer?"

"Yeah, Bauer. Jack Bauer's sister." She turned to Liddell. "Maybe you don't remember Jack, Liddell. He
was Russo's accountant."

Liddell nodded. "Committed suicide."

"He was murdered," the redhead spat out. "Sure, it
was a good job, but I'd been hearing from Jack regularly. He was getting ready to turn Russo's books over
to the Feds. So he had to die."

"You're crazy. I should have known there was something phony about you—" Russo stared at her bale-
fully.

Chilly shook her head. "There was nothing phony.
I was only a kid when Jack died. But from then on, I
worked at being Chilly, the kind of a girl Tony Russo
would go for. Just so I could get next to you. And get
even for Jack."

Russo's voice was low. "Get her out of here, Liddell,
and keep her away from me. Anything happens to me,
she'll fry for it. I promise you."

On the floor, Maxie was groaning his way back to
consciousness. Liddell took the redhead by the arm,
stepped across Maxie, led her to the door.

"You'll get my bill in the mail," Liddell told Russo.
He cut off the stream of obscenities by slamming the
door behind them.

The pounding on the door sounded like the rattle of
a machine gun. Johnny Liddell groaned, started to
roll over, collided with the back of a sofa. He opened
his eyes, looked around at the unfamiliar furnishing.
After a moment, he identified his whereabouts as

Chilly's apartment. The man pounding on the door seemed on the verge of breaking it down.

Chilly peeked her head around the doorway leading to the bedroom. She turned wide, frightened eyes on Liddell.

"Russo's men?" she whispered.

Liddell shrugged. He slid his feet onto the floor. He reached for the holster hung over the back of the chair, tugged out the .45.

"You'd better get into the bathroom. Let me handle it." He waited until she ran for the bathroom door, a sheet wrapped around her, then he crossed to the living-room door, unlocked it and pulled it open.

The man in the hallway dropped his eyes to the .45 that was pointed at his middle, then the cold eyes traveled up to Liddell's face.

"Well, fancy meeting you here."

Liddell pursed his lips, let the gun drop to his side. "Come on in, Inspector." He stepped aside, watched Inspector Herlehy stalk into the room, slammed the door shut in the face of the curious tenants in other flats who lined their doorways in varying stages of undress.

Herlehy stopped inside the room, swung on Liddell, hands on hips. "What are you doing here?" He looked around. "And where's the girl?"

"I've been bedded down out here in the living room. She's sleeping in there. In the bedroom." He nodded toward the bedroom door. The inspector started toward it, Liddell beat him to it, blocked the way. "You haven't shown me that little piece of paper that gives you the right to go barging like this, Inspector. Or are you running the Morals Squad now?"

The white-haired man studied him with grim eyes, shook his head. "Still Homicide. And if you insist on technicalities, maybe we can provide transportation down to headquarters to discuss this."

Liddell shook his head. "I'll get her out here." He walked into the bedroom, tapped on the bathroom door. "Get decent. Police are here and it looks like trouble."

There was a slight pause, then a muffled, "Be right out."

Liddell picked up his shirt, was shrugging into it when he walked back into the living room. The inspector was on the telephone, just finishing a conversation. He dropped the receiver back on its hook.

"Just calling off an APB on both you and the girl," Herlehy grunted. "You really went away out this time, didn't you, shamus?"

"You still haven't told me what it's all about," Liddell complained. He laid the .45 on the coffee table, stuck the tails of his shirt into his waistband.

Herlehy picked up the gun, held the muzzle to his nose, dropped the .45 into his pocket. "That's right. I haven't," the inspector said. "You got anything to tell me?"

The door to the bedroom opened, the redhead walked out, tying a blue silk robe around her waist. Her eyes sought Liddell's questioningly.

"What is it, Johnny?"

Liddell shrugged. He nodded to Herlehy. "This is Inspector Herlehy of Homicide. Best I can guess is he's working for Doc Kinsey on his time off."

"How long you been here, Miss Conover?"

Her eyes sought Johnny's again. "Since about two. We left the club and came right here—"

Herlehy turned to Liddell. "And you?"

"I'm with her, Inspector. You going to tell us what happened?"

Herlehy raked at his white hair. "Tony Russo was gunned out tonight in his office. Shot through the back of the head." He turned frosty blue eyes on the girl. "He'd been getting some notes, threatening to kill him. Know anything about them?"

The girl caught her lower lip between her teeth, started to answer, was waved to silence by Liddell. "Sure, she knows all about them. She sent them. But

Russo was alive when we left him and I haven't left her since."

"That's true, Inspector. He was alive when we left," Chilly put in. "I—was scared, so I asked Johnny to stay here with me in case Russo tried something."

Herlehy squinted at Liddell. "But you slept out here, you said."

"I'll still testify that she didn't leave me tonight."

"It's not good enough, Johnny. The D.A.'s smart enough to see that any alibi like that is self-serving. It not only gives her one, but it gives you one, too."

"Why should I kill the bum?"

Herlehy stared at a discolored bruise on the private detective's jaw. "Maybe because he set one of his goons on you and worked you over."

"That goon was eating the carpet when we left. I had nothing against Russo. He owes me money, matter of fact. Why should I kill him?"

"We're not saying you did. But we are saying your friend here might have. I'll have to take you both downtown."

Liddell started to protest, read the message in the older man's eye, shrugged. "You're making a big mistake, Inspector."

"I hope you didn't make a bigger one—killing that rat."

Johnny Liddell sat in the ante-chamber of the assistant district attorney assigned to homicide. He wondered in which of the other ante-chambers they were holding the redhead. He hadn't seen her since the policewoman had taken charge of her at headquarters.

He shifted uncomfortably on the hard wooden bench, checked his wristwatch. It was almost 10 o'clock when the assistant D.A. pulled open his door, walked out into the ante-chamber.

"Sorry to keep you waiting, Liddell." Maury Lovin had had plenty of contact with the private detective in the ten years he'd put in as an assistant. Now that he was within grabbing distance of the Big Boss's office, Levin wasn't about to make any enemies. Certainly not one who'd been so helpful to his boss on numerous occasions and whose help Levin himself might conceivably need some day soon. "Had to check you out."

"And?"

Levin shrugged, raised his hands, palms upward. "Clean. Ballistics cleared your gun, we don't have any motive that would stand up in court. You're free to go."

"And the girl?"

Levin pursed his lips judiciously. "That's a different story, Johnny. The Big Boss wants her held. She had motive, she had opportunity, she had everything."

"I tell you she wasn't out of my sight all night."

"I know you and I trust you. The grand jury doesn't. They're going to want a lot more than your word when those letters are read in court and the jury hears about her brother." He squinted at Liddell. "If you were to come up with another suspect—" He shrugged. "You know my door is always open to you, Johnny."

"What about my gun?"

"Property clerk will give you a release on it."

Liddell swung on his heel, stamped out of the office. As soon as the door had slammed behind him, Inspector Herlehy joined Levin in the doorway to the ante-room. The assistant D.A. turned a worried look on the white-haired man. "I hope he realizes the license he has for that gun isn't a hunting license."

Herlehy shook his head. "He does. He wants the killer alive. Just like we do. If we start digging into Russo's setup, there'll be plenty of heat for a cover-up. Nobody ever invented enough heat to stop Liddell."

Johnny Liddell dropped the cab at the entrance to the morgue, just across the street from the pile of bricks and acres of glass windows that go to make up Bellevue Hospital. This is the last port of call for the fashionable suicide from Beekman Towers as well as

for the pitiable bundle of rags that slept away its life
in a Bowery doorway. Here they sleep, side by side, the
one whose passing rated 96-point headlines in the tabs
and the one whose passing was completely unnoticed
except by those who demanded its removal from their
doorway as a nuisance.

Liddell walked down the short stairway to the old-
fashioned elevator cage. He rode it to the basement,
clanged back the heavy door, walked to the door stenciled *Examining Room*. He knocked, pushed open the
door. A thin little wisp of a woman sat behind the
desk. She nodded toward an unmarked door. "The doc-
tor's expecting you inside."

Inside the other room, two white-frocked men were
leaning over a half-covered body on a sandstone examining table. The older of the two straightened up,
nodded to Liddell as he joined them.

On the table Tony Russo lay on his back, staring up
at the overhead light with eyes that would never see
again. His hair was wet, dank, washed back from his
face. His neck was supported by a notched wood-block.
The canvas was rolled down far enough to expose
the large x-shaped sutures that signaled the fact that
an autopsy was already under way.

"Thanks for letting me see him, doc," Liddell told
the older of the two men. "I wanted to have a look
at the wound myself."

The man in the white smock put his fingers against
the dead man's temple, pushed the head to show a
small hole behind the left ear. "Went in there." He
straightened the head, showed a larger, ragged hole
under the right jaw. "Came out here. Powder burns
at the point of entry indicate the killer was standing
right behind him." He unhooked a clipboard from the
side of the table, ran his eyes over the penciled nota-
tions. "Time of death approximately 2 a.m.—give or
take fifteen minutes. Gun was a .32." He rolled his
eyes up from the clipboard. "That's about all we have
until the results of the P.M. are posted."

"Not much doubt about what killed him, is there?"

The white-frocked man shrugged, hung the clipboard back on its hook. "If that slug behind the ear didn't kill him, it's a cinch it didn't add to his chances of breaking ninety," he grunted. He stared down at the gray features of the dead man. "At that, he lasted a lot longer than I'd figure him for. We've processed a lot of his friends through here. And even more of his enemies."

Johnny nodded, started to turn away.

"Funny that when he did get it, he'd get it from a girl, huh, Johnny?" the man in white continued.

Liddell turned around. "Chilly Conover?" He shook his head. "She didn't do it."

The lab man shrugged. "Sorry. I didn't know it was like that. But you ought to get her to level with you if you're going out on a limb for her."

"Meaning?"

"The gun. It belongs to her. And she was seen going up to Russo's office around that time."

"I was in there at the time. He sent for her and—"

"Not this time. The guy who saw her heading for Russo's office says you were in the lobby making passes at the hatcheck girl. You were there almost twenty minutes. The hatchick will back it up."

A worried frown etched a V between Liddell's brows. He nodded. "Thanks for the tip, doc. I'll do as much some time."

He turned, walked toward the small hallway leading to the elevator. Some things that had been puzzling him were beginning to get clear. Too clear!

Maury Levin, the assistant D.A., sat behind his heavily piled desk, played with a pencil. His eyes were wary, he wore a worried frown.

"You could really jam me up, Liddell. I'm counting on you playing this one with no curves."

"Haven't I always?"

Levin nodded. There was a knock on the door, a

uniformed patrolman stuck his head in. "She's in Interrogation C, Mr. Levin."

The assistant D.A. nodded, the cop's head was withdrawn.

"In C, Johnny. You've got ten minutes."

"I'll only need one, Maury." He headed for the
doorway, slammed the door after him.

Interrogation C was halfway down the hallway between Maury Levin's office and the double glass doors
leading to the Big Boss's private office. The redhead
was sitting on a hard-backed wooden chair, twisting
her handkerchief nervously between her fingers. She
jumped to her feet as Liddell walked in, ran to him.

A policewoman, seated by the screen-meshed window, got up, walked to the door. "I'll be outside, Mr.
Liddell. You understand you have only ten minutes."

Liddell nodded, waited until she had closed the door
behind her. Then, as he turned back to the redhead,
she tried to find his mouth with hers. He pushed her
out at arm's length, her eyes widened with fear.

"You went up to Tony Russo's office while I was
waiting for you to clean out your dressing room, didn't
you?" Before she could interrupt, he continued, "You
used the private elevator, took a gun to make good
those crazy threats."

"No. I—"

"And you used me for a patsy. I was going to be
able to swear you were with me every minute."

The resistance seemed to drain out of the girl. She
went limp, he dropped her into the chair.

"You think I killed him, too. You think I'm a—"

"What I think about you doesn't matter. It's what
the D.A. is going to make a jury think about you that
does."

She shook her head. "I didn't kill him, Johnny." She
caught at his sleeve. "I won't lie to you. I did go up
there with a gun, I wanted to see him crawl. Just once
more." She shook her head. "But he was too much for
me. He took the gun away from me and he told he he'd

kill me if he ever saw me again. But I didn't kill him, Johnny."

"Anybody see you leave? Maxie or any of his boys?"

Chilly shook her head. "I didn't see them."

"So there's no one can prove Russo was still alive when you left?"

"He was. The first I knew about him being dead was when that policeman broke into my place. You've got to believe me, Johnny." She dropped her hand from his sleeve. "I know I have no right to expect you to help after I held out on you—"

Liddell walked to the door, rapped. The policewoman eyed them with surprise, checked her watch. "You still have eight minutes."

Liddell grinned at her. "Too long to talk and not long enough not to talk." He turned back to the redhead. "Sit tight until you hear from me."

Chilly worked at a smile with questionable success. She looked around the room, her eyes coming to stop on the policewoman. "It doesn't look as if I'm going to have much of a choice."

An hour later, Johnny Liddell ran up the short flight of steps leading into Stillson's Gym, dropped a quarter in the turnstile and pushed through. A thick fog of cigar smoke swirled lazily near the ceiling of the room. The heavy smell of liniment and perspiration was something tangible. A low hum of conversation was spiced with the rhythmic chatter of punching bags, the scuffing of skipping feet, the thud of punches on the heavy bags.

Liddell stood in the entrance, looked around. In the center of the floor a huge Negro, wearing ear guards, was boxing listlessly with an old chopping block, sharpening his right. Around the wall, house fighters and prelim boys were working out on the pulleys, shadow boxing, feinting and weaving or skipping a rope tirelessly.

Johnny walked over to the ring. In the Negro's corner, a fat man, his fedora shoved on the back of his head, a cold cigar clenched in the corner of his mouth scowled as he watched the men in the ring. He wore no coat, dried half-moons of sweat stained the under-arms of the shirt he wore. He checked his stopwatch, signaled for an end to the round.

"Get him under a shower," he growled at a rubber. He turned, nodded to Liddell. "Hello, Johnny. Long time." He pulled the cold cigar from between his teeth. "No trouble, I hope?"

Liddell shook his head. "No trouble. I just wanted to have a talk with Maxie Hughes. He usually works out down here, don't he?"

The fat man grunted, returned the cigar unlit to his mouth. He squinted as he glanced around the room, shoved a stubby thumb in the direction of the heavy bags. "Every day. Like clockwork. You'd think the bum was going someplace. Thinks he's still got it."

"He had his day."

The fat man made a face. "With Russo calling the plays? Even I could be champ like that. He says dive, you dive. You don't dive, don't go reading continued stories. You know?" He removed the cigar, spat in a bucket. "Russo makes. He makes good. But a slob like that?" He hunched his shoulders. "Walks on his heels and he ain't got the what-with to buy a decent meal." He glanced back at Liddell. "Say, that what you want to see him about? Russo?"

Liddell considered for a moment, decided to play it straight. "Yeah. They're cooling a client of mine for the job. She says she didn't do it. I figure Maxie might be able to help me clear her."

"I wish you luck." The fat man pulled his fedora down over his eyes. "Anyway, let me know when the collection's being taken. I want in."

"The collection?"

"Yeah. To buy your client a medal for chilling that louse." He turned, shuffled in the direction of the show-ers. Liddell watched him thoughtfully for a moment, then walked over to where Maxie was grunting with every punch he threw at the heavy bag.

The cue-ball head glistened with a thin sheen of sweat; his chest was covered with heavy caracul-like hair. Mounds of muscles sat along his shoulder line and biceps like knots. He held the big bag to a stop as Liddell walked up, stopped near him. Unconsciously, he touched his gloved hand tenderly to his mashed nose.

"That was a lucky one you hit me with last night, shamus," he growled. "Real lucky."

Liddell shrugged. "Like you said, nothing personal." He dug into his pockets, brought up a pack of cigarettes, held it out to Maxie, drew a shake of the head. "Tough about your boss."

Maxie shrugged, bit at the knots on his glove, got it open. "I was fixing to go back to the ring anyhow." He slipped the glove off his hand, flexed his fingers, untied the other glove. "I still got some good years in me."

"You couldn't even get a prelim go at St. Nick's and you know it," Liddell told him coldly. "You're not only a has-been. You're a never-was, Maxie. The only reason you kept winning is because Russo saw to it you did."

"You're a liar," the bald-headed man roared.

"You've got a glass jaw and a debutante could flatten you with that lard belly—"

Maxie looked around, dropped his voice. His eyes were narrowed, piglike. "You're trying to make me mad, shamus. Only I'm too smart to fall for it. Get going and keep going."

Liddell touched a light to the cigarette. "When you killed him, you killed your only chance to eat regularly—"

"Me kill him?" Maxie shook his head. "The redhead killed him. She kept sending him notes saying she was going to, and she finally did."

"So you weren't out cold? You heard Russo accuse her of sending the notes. It gave you an idea, didn't it, Maxie?"

The battered face twisted into a caricature of a smile. "You going to prove something, shamus?"

"Yeah. I'm going to prove Chilly went back there last night with a gun—"

The bald head bobbed delightedly. "The cops already know that. It was her gun that killed him—"

"They also know Russo took the gun away from her and threw her out." Some of the grin on Maxie's face faded. "But you didn't know that, because you weren't there—where you were supposed to be."

The eyes were. narrowed again. Maxie licked at his thickened lips. "You're lying."

Liddell shook his head. "You already had two strikes on you. I made you eat carpet. Russo didn't like that. When you're not on the door where you're supposed to be, and you let the girl get at him again—you struck out."

The pig eyes darted around the room. "Who'd listen to you? They know you got the hots for the broad and—"

"The gun was lying there on the desk when he threw you out, wasn't it?" He blocked Maxie as the ex-pug started to walk away. "But you made two mistakes, Maxie. Two big ones!"

"You're trying to pull something, Liddell. You don't make me admit a thing. And you can't prove anything."

"I don't have to, Maxie. Didn't you know they already gave Chilly the nitrate test?" He shook his head. "Negative."

"What are you talking about?"

"The nitrate test. It tells whether you've fired a gun or not recently. The gun kicks back tiny particles of powder. Then they make a paraffin cast of your hand. If you fired a gun recently, they'll be there."

Maxie fought a losing battle to keep his eyes off his right hand.

"It stays for three, maybe four days. Even if you wash your hands a dozen times. It'll be there when they check your hand." He watched the play of emotions on the other man's face. "You made another mistake, Maxie."

The piglike eyes rolled up from the hand to the detective's face. "Russo was scared of Chilly. He never would have let her get in back of him. You—he had nothing but contempt for you. Always did have."

"I was a champ."

"A cheese champ. And he made you. Now he was throwing you to the wolves. Didn't care if you ended up selling pencils in the lobby at the Garden, did he, Maxie?"

Maxie licked at his lips. "He was a nothing. I was the champ."

"He never let you forget how you got to be champ, did he, Maxie?" Liddell could feel the perspiration forming in beads on his forehead and upper lip. "When he fired you last night he told you all about it, didn't he? Laughed at you."

Maxie wiped his mouth with the back of his arm. "I made him a million. Because I was the champ. I made him a million."

"And he was going to throw you out."

Maxie seemed to be focusing his eyes yards behind Liddell's head. "I told him how it felt to be champ. He laughed at me." He hit his chest with the side of his hand. "He said I was champ of the tankers. That I never won a fair go in my life." The eyes came back to Liddell's face. "That's a lie. You know it's a lie."

Liddell dropped the cigarette to the floor, crushed it out. He put his hand into his jacket pocket. The butt of the gun had a cold reassuring feel.

"He told me if I was so good, to go make it on my own. Then he told me to get out before he had me thrown out." The absent look was back in the eyes. "He turned and walked away from me. I went after him, you know? Just to reason with him." He shook his head as though he was having difficulty understanding. "The gun was there. I grabbed it. And that's all I remember."

Liddell's voice was gentle. "Nobody can blame you, Maxie. But you're going to have to tell them about it. Downtown." For an anxious moment, his fingers tightened on the butt of the gun.

Then Maxie nodded. "Okay, Johnny. If you say so."

Johnny Liddell sprawled in the chair across the desk from Maury Levin, watched the assistant D.A. read the flimsy, nod at the signature on the bottom. "All signed, sealed and delivered." He looked over to where Inspector Herlehy stood at the window, staring out into the park below. "You satisfied, Inspector?"

Herlehy shrugged. "The confession stands up." He cast a baleful glare at Liddell. "I'm too smart to ask you how you got it."

Liddell grinned. "I'll be glad to explain—"

Herlehy held his hand up. "Never mind. I don't want to be an accessory to it, whatever it is." He turned at a knock on the door.

"Come in," Levin directed.

The door opened, Chilly Conover walked in. Her eyes hopscotched around the room, came to rest on Johnny. She walked over to him. "I just heard, Johnny. I don't know how I'll ever thank you."

Liddell winked at the assistant D.A., got up, took the redhead by the arm, piloted her to the door. With his hand on the knob, he turned and grinned at the inspector. "Any time you need my help, Inspector—"

"Get out before I remember some law I can book you under," the white-haired man roared.

Liddell ushered Chilly into the corridor, followed her and closed the door after them.

Maury Levin sat at his desk, laced his fingers behind his head, stared at the door dreamily. "What a lucky guy! She says she don't know how she'll ever thank him."

Herlehy grunted. "If I know Liddell—she'll find a way."

Dead Run

He was a big man. He lay on his back, his head twisted to the side. An elaborate hairpiece sat askew his head, dislodged by what must have been a violent wrench.

A purple-black hole under his cheekbone had spilled a red cascade down the side of his face to stain his collar. A larger hole that fed the red puddle under his face showed where the slug had come through the top of his skull.

He had once been handsome, but time and a thin layer of fat had softened the clean lines of his profile. His skin had the appearance of having been well and frequently massaged to slow up the devastation of time. Dave Trellis wouldn't have to worry any more about the oncoming of old age. The slug through his skull made it pretty definite that he wouldn't grow any older.

Johnny Liddell stood back, watched the tech men from Homicide go through their paces. The little man at his side, almost submerged in the heavily padded shoulders he normally affected, seemed to have shrunk even more. He was busily macerating the cuticle on his thumb when Inspector Herlehy of Homicide walked away from the dead man, came over to where they stood.

The inspector favored Liddell with a look that showed no signs of enthusiasm. He looked past him to the thin man.

"Let's go over this again, Lewis—"

The thin man managed to look even unhappier. "I gave everything I know to that cop over there, and—"

"Suppose you give it to me," Herlehy snapped.

Marty Lewis bobbed his head. "Sure, sure. I just didn't want for you to go wasting your time. I—"

Herlehy consulted some scribbled notes. "You're Marty Lewis. You were Trellis's press agent. Right?" Herlehy didn't wait for corroboration. He glanced up at Liddell. "You sent for Liddell. Why?"

"I got a feeling I'm going to need some help."

Herlehy rolled his eyes from Liddell to Lewis. "You mean you don't think the department is capable of catching the killer. So you brought in a specialist."

The press agent detected the snide note in the inspector's tone. "It's not that, Inspector. It's just that— well, there are some things about this kill that are going to look funny—"

Herlehy turned back to where two men were transferring Trellis's body to a stretcher. "I'll bet. He looks like he died laughing." He brought his scowl back to the little man. "Try me. I haven't had a good laugh all day."

"It ain't that kind of funny." Lewis shook his head. "Peculiar more. You know?"

"Go on."

The press agent sighed deeply, turned beseeching eyes on Johnny Liddell who picked that moment to get interested in a stain on the ceiling. "Well—you remember Trellis. He was real big in Hollywood maybe twenty, twenty-five years ago." He looked hopefully to the inspector for encouragement, got none, plowed on hurriedly. "He's been out of the business ever since. Now he's getting set to stage a comeback. You know?"

Herlehy shook his head. "Don't tell me this is a publicity stunt?"

Lewis looked devastated, took a deep breath, then bobbed his head. "Yes, sir, Inspector. That's just what it is. A publicity stunt."

"Well, your boy's going to get lots of space," Herlehy conceded. "But he's not going to be reading it. Not unless he uses a ouija board." He squinted at the little man. "Tell me about this publicity stunt."

The press agent swallowed nervously; his Adam's apple bobbed and quivered. "Trellis figured he creamed the ladies. You know, like in the old days when he did all those big movies with Rita Melott. So he figured when we booked him at the club—"

"What club?"

"The Artists and Models on 54th Street."

"Bunty Carter's place, huh?"

"Wait a minute, Inspector," Lewis put in hastily. "Bunty's got no piece of this action. This was strictly between Trellis and me. Look, don't drag Bunty in. He'll—"

"Get back to the story," Herlehy told him coldly.

Lewis dug a balled handkerchief from his pocket, swabbed at his face. "Like I was saying, Trellis wanted me to build up the romance and glamour bit—you know, bill him as America's King of Romance. That kind of jazz." The balled handkerchief did another circuit of his face. "Hell, most of the people making the scene today hardly remember him. And those that do, they know that King of Romance bit is for the birds. Who's gonna buy a guy his age as glamorous or romantic?"

"So?"

"So he says take a look around. Clark Gable—Cary Grant—any of those guys, they ain't exactly kids and go that route all right. I try to talk him out of it. He's no Gable or Grant or even John Wayne, I tell him. Besides, those guys got their own hair and they catnip the dames every time they open their mouths. That's when he comes up with the idea."

"What idea?"

Lewis looked to Johnny Liddell for help, got nothing but a bland stare in return. "We're going to build him up as a guy who catnips the dames." The press agent sighed softly. "He picks a kid from the line, a real dish named Kitty Mallon. A friend of Johnny's—"

Herlehy snorted. "She would be." He scribbled the

name in his notebook, glared at Liddell. "If you figure that gives you a pass to stick your nose into this—"

Liddell shook his head. "I'm just a friendly ob-
server."

"Stay that way," the inspector snorted. He turned
back to Lewis. "Let's hear this inspiration that was
going to turn your boy into the great lover."

"Trellis figures that if some real sex wagon flips
over him, the other women will figure he's got something and flip, too. So the gag was for Mallon to really
do the big-eyed bit for him." He shrugged. "If you
read the columns, you'll know they went for it hook,
line and sinker. You pick up a paper the last couple of
weeks and from the play he's been getting you'd think
Dave Trellis had a corner on the Wheaties crop."

"What was in it for this"—he consulted the written
notes—"this Kitty Mallon?"

"Publicity. Name in the columns, picture in the
paper. It all helps."

Herlehy signaled one of the plainclothesmen to his
side. Then he turned back to Lewis. "This Kitty Mallon. Got an address?"

Lewis licked at his lips. "I—"

A harsh note crept into Herlehy's voice. "I told
you from the beginning, Lewis. I expect full co-opera-
tion. If I don't get it—"

The press agent bobbed his head. He pulled a worn
leather address book from his pocket. He riffled
through the pages, found the notation. "She lives in
the Morris Arms on 49th Street. Apartment 2C."

Herlehy turned to the plainclothesman. "I want her
in my office right away, Ray." The detective nodded,
headed for the door. Herlehy turned back, stared at
Liddell and the press agent soberly. "I don't know
what you're supposed to be doing here, Johnny, but
I don't want any monkeyshines. And you, Lewis—stay
around where I can lay my hands on you."

Lewis nodded.

"And me, Inspector?" Liddell wanted to know.

"You? You can go any place you like. In fact, if you'd like a suggestion—"

"No, thanks. I've got a good imagination."

The inspector turned on his heel, headed for the door. Bill Nagel, his driver, grinned at Liddell, winked as he followed Herlehy out of the apartment. As soon as the door closed, Liddell whirled on Lewis.

"What was the idea of giving him her address?"

"What's the difference? She's not there."

"How do you know?"

Lewis looked around, lowered his voice. "When I called you, I called her, too. I got her stashed away in a riding academy on 47th Street. Room 604 in the Sherwood. You know the place?"

Liddell wrinkled his nose. "Doesn't everybody?"

"So what'd you want me to do," the press agent asked in a hurt tone, "stick her in the Plaza or something?" He wiped at his forehead. "Reason I had to see you, Johnny, there was something I didn't tell you. About the setup."

"What?"

"The romance bit was supposed to be built up to a payoff. Payoff comes just before his opening when he starts giving her the go-by. She's supposed to write him a letter—" The little man licked at his lips. "She tells him if she can't have him, nobody else can."

Liddell groaned. "She wrote the letter?"

"I asked her. It went out last night."

Liddell eyed the lab men who were desultorily powdering for prints, lowered his voice. "We've got to find it."

"I already looked as much as I could before the cops got here. It's gone." The tip of his tongue flicked at his lips. "Johnny, you got to help us crack this one—fast."

"I'll do the best I can."

"You got to do even better. It's not good for my

business when people stop reading the names of my
clients in gossip columns and start reading them in
obituary columns. You know?"

Broadway is a tired old street, living in the glamour
of its past, ignoring the fact that its present is wrapped
up in orange-juice stands, bookstores specializing in
cut-rate pornography and record stores that spill nerve-
jangling rhythm out onto its sidewalks. Where once
glamorous showgirls and their Johns paraded to their
favorite supper club, now duck-tailed hoods, underage
hustlers, perverts and queers tirelessly prowl its side
streets at all hours of the day and night.

Johnny Liddell came up out of the subway entrance
at the corner of 42nd Street and Broadway. He stood
on the corner for a moment, apparently staring down
the once fabulous street that now specializes in grind
movies, flea circuses, army and navy stores and all degrees of degeneracy—both male and female. Actually,
he was watching the subway entrance for some evidence
of a tail.

When he was finally satisfied that no one had followed him from the subway, he melted into the stream
of gaping tourists, chattering Puerto Ricans, hoods
and would-be hoods, panhandlers and pushers who've
taken over the Times Square area as their own. He let
the tide carry him toward 47th Street. As he crossed
the pigeon-limed island that separates Broadway from
Seventh Avenue in front of the Palace, he looked up
at the statue of the Fighting 69th's Father Duffy. He
wondered what the padre must be thinking as his eyes
watched the changes in the Great White Way in the
few years his statue had been standing there. 47th
Street between Seventh and Sixth is known as Dream
Street. You can buy any kind of a dream in most of
the mean, soot-stained buildings that line both sides
of the street—from a cloud 7 to a nightmare.

Liddell walked into the drugstore on the corner, slid
on a stool and ordered coffee from a fluttery creature

behind the counter. He looked around, waited for
some sign that he had been tailed. A brassy blonde
at the far end of the counter studied him speculatively,
smiled tentatively around the cigarette she held between her lips. It was hardly evening—and already
Dream Street was putting its merchandise on display.

Liddell's eyes slid past her and the interest faded
from her eyes. He watched the Broadway entrance to
the store, moved his elbow so the counter man could
slide a cup of coffee in front of him. When he was
satisfied no one was watching him, Liddell dropped
some change next to the untouched coffee, walked
to the side door of the store and emerged on 47th
Street.

The Sherwood was an old stone building, nestled
anonymously in a row of similar old stone buildings.
It stared out onto Dream Street through two large,
grimy plate-glass windows which removed any doubt
of its character by the words *Hotel Sherwood* stenciled
across each.

The lobby was small, dark. A counter with a key
rack was against the back wall, presided over by a
small man with a perpetually runny nose and rheumy
eyes. He offered no objection as Liddell passed up the
desk, crossed the worn carpet which showed its backing through the cracks. Instead, he played the game he
usually played this early in the evening—tried to re-
call which was the last girl in—the one who was making the first kill of the evening. Later on, the Johns
appeared with such frequency that he couldn't keep
count—but this early it was always a good game to pass
the time. Irritably he finally acknowledged that she
must have slipped past him. He couldn't remember
any of the girls returning.

Liddell rode the creaking self-service elevator to the
sixth floor, followed the discolored runner to 604. He
put his ear to the door, knocked softly. There was a
brief pause, then. "Yes?"

He looked up and down the hallway, lowered his voice. "Liddell."

There was a sound of a key turning in the lock, the door opened a crack. When she'd satisfied herself who it was, Kitty Mallon opened the door, stood aside while Liddell slipped through.

The room was small, facing on the blank brick wall of another building. A half-open door led to a lavatory with a cracked mirror. The bed was turned down, showed its dingy linen. The only light in the room was a bridge lamp that spilled a yellow triangle over a sag-bottomed chair.

"I'm so glad you got here, Johnny," the girl told him. "I've been going crazy since Marty called." She was tall—the show girl type—her thick, coppery hair was mussed, the color had drained from her face leaving it murky in the light of the lamp. She wore a tight pair of velvet toreadors, a thin blouse that gave ample evidence that she needed no artificial embellishment to the magnificence of her façade. "How's it look?"

Liddell considered, shrugged. "Not good. Trellis is dead and the police want to talk to you."

"Why? I had nothing to do with him."

"You kidding? I've been reading all about you and this antediluvian wolf. So has everyone else."

"But it was just publicity. Marty planted those items."

"And this letter you wrote him?"

"Also part of the build-up." She dropped in the chair, nervously dry-washed her hands. "Johnny, I know how it all looks. But I swear to you—I had nothing to do with him. Who'd believe that letter, Johnny? Trellis was old enough to be my father—and that ridiculous hairpiece made me—"

"The papers believed it enough to run the items," Liddell reminded her. "Herlehy will believe it enough to book you. If he finds the letter."

"If?"

Liddell nodded. "Marty says the letter was gone

when he found the body. That means one of two things —either the killer took it with him, in which case we get a breather; or Trellis stuck it some place and Herlehy's men will find it sooner or later. In which case, we've got to move and move fast."

The girl's hands were busy in her lap again. "I don't even know where we're going to turn."

"Leave that up to me." Liddell sat on the edge of the unmade bed. "You've been seeing quite a lot of Trellis during the past couple of weeks. Think hard. Did you ever see anything or hear anything that could help?"

The redhead caught her full upper lip between her teeth, worried it for a moment, shook her head. "Nothing I can remember."

"How about any of the places you've been?"

She shook her head again. "The usual places. You know, places where we could be seen. We—" She broke off for a moment, frowned. "There was one place he wouldn't go. The Show Place. You know—the cellar joint on 46th Street."

"Harry Nast's joint. Got a wheel and a dice setup in the back. I know the place." He brought a pack of cigarettes from his pocket, held it out to the girl. "Why wouldn't he go there?"

She shrugged, put the cigarette between her lips, leaned forward to accept a light. "I don't know. He just wouldn't." She took a deep drag, let the smoke dribble from between parted lips. "I wanted to because I know most of the big-time columnists make the place. I figured it would be a natural—" She took another drag on the cigarette, settled back in the chair. "He was paying the tariff, so I figured it was up to him to name the route."

Liddell nodded, lit his own cigarette. "Anything else?"

"Just the words he had with Bunty at the club."

"What about?"

The redhead shrugged. "It was nothing, really.

Bunty took a long shot by signing Trellis. After all these years, he was pretty much of a nothing. Then when all the publicity starts to break, Trellis starts beefing that Bunty should be paying him a lot more. You know, the usual beef from a ham."

"What happened?"

The redhead shrugged. "Bunty laid it right on the line. He'd picked Trellis up when he was flat on his back and gave him his chance. He was going to get first crack at anything Dave did." She took a deep drag on the cigarette, took it from between her lips, studied the carmined end. "Trellis was bluffing and Bunty called it. Nobody else in town would touch him. He was good for maybe a freak three-week stand—and then back where he came from. Nowheresville."

Liddell nodded. "This payoff—when you were supposed to make sure no one else had him. What about it?"

The redhead made a moue of distaste. "It was real cornball, Johnny. I was supposed to make a pest of myself, bust into his apartment, threaten to kill him if he left me." She tried to take the taste out of her mouth with smoke, didn't quite make it. "By the time the house dick broke in, he'd have me billing and cooing. You make the picture?"

"I'm trying not to."

Kitty nodded, managed a grin. "They tell me careers have been built with less."

"Not recently," Liddell grunted. "This gun. Got it?"

Deep lines creased a V between the girl's brows. "No. I looked for it after Marty called. It's gone." She shrugged. "I may have mislaid it, or left it in my dressing table at the club. But I don't think so."

"What kind of a gun was it?"

"A .32."

Liddell walked to the phone, dialed a number. He waited while it rang, the redhead smoked with short, nervous puffs. Then, "Give me Lieutenant Michaels in Ballistics, will you?"

After a moment, "Mike? Johnny Liddell."

The voice on the other end was slow, drawling. "What's on your mind, Johnny?"

"Mike, get anything on that Dave Trellis kill?"

Michaels grunted. "Hell, whoever did that sure was wasting his time. Give that old creep a couple more days and he'd have died of old age." He paused for a second. "What'd you want to know?"

"Got any idea of the caliber?"

"Hard to tell without an autopsy."

Liddell snorted. "You saw the entry wound. What do you make it?"

Michaels considered. "Got better than that, Johnny. One of my boys found the slug. Too bashed up for a make, but I'd say it was pretty sure to be a .32. Weighs out that way."

Liddell nodded. "Thanks, Mike." He dropped the receiver, stared at it for a moment.

"A .32?" the redhead asked quietly.

Liddell nodded.

"I'm in a spot. Right?" she asked. She didn't wait for his nod, but got up and walked over to him. "You've got to help me, Johnny."

"That's what I'm here for."

She slid her arms around his neck, stood on her tiptoes and pasted her mouth against his. He could feel her lips moving, her body warm and close. As he pulled her even closer, she slid out of his arms.

"Not now." Her breath was coming unevenly, her eyes sparkled. "I just wanted you to remember what you were working for."

The chairs in the Show Place were piled on the table, a man with an apron was doing a half-hearted job of chasing the dust around the floor. At a back table, two men, their gray fedoras on the backs of their heads, were playing gin.

Johnny Liddell walked in, blinked at the dimness in the room, waited until his eyes adjusted themselves to the change from the bright sunlight outside. Neither of the two men looked up as he crossed the room to them.

"Harry around?" he asked.

The slimmer of the two men reached over, picked a three of diamonds from the pile, fitted it into his hand. He discarded a six of clubs. The other man scowled, reached for it. Liddell swung his hand in a half arc, sent the pack flying to the floor.

The man who'd been reaching for the discard looked up. There was no trace of anger in his face, merely interest. "We got company, Allie," he told the slim man.

Allie looked up, squinted at Liddell. His face was thin, seemed thinner because of his hooked nose and high cheekbones. His mouth was a thin, bloodless slit, his hair was thick where it showed under the tilted fedora.

"What do you want?"

"Harry Nast," Liddell told him. When the thin man showed no signs of moving, Liddell kicked out. His foot connected with the side of the chair, sent the thin man sprawling.

The other man was on his feet, got up just in time to field a haymaker with his midsection. As the air wheezed out of his lungs, Liddell brought up a looping right that sent him staggering backwards. He landed on a table, chairs and tables collapsed under his weight. He lay there in the wreckage, sucking air noisily into his lungs.

"Just a minute, Liddell." Allie sat on the floor, a .45 looking the size of a cannon in his fist. His finger was white on the trigger, his hand shaking with repressed anger. "Give me an excuse. Any excuse."

"Nast won't like it, Allie," Liddell told him. "That might bring the cops. The cops might stumble onto that back room. And you'd look silly as hell walking across the East River with a pair of cement overshoes on."

The thin man glared, pulled himself to his feet. "You all right, Vince?" he called to the other man.

The answer was a half-strangled grunt as the bigger man struggled to pull himself out of the tangle of smashed tables and chairs. He finally managed to get to his feet, stood swaying, his hands laced across his midsection.

"What do we do with him?" Allie wanted to know.

"He's right about one thing," Vince growled. "Harry'd flip if you cooled him here. We can't stand any heat." He wiped his mouth with the back of his hand. "We better let Harry decide."

Liddell grinned pleasantly. "Now that's what I've been trying to tell you all along. I want to see Harry Nast."

The door to the gaming room was the back wall of two phone booths in the rear of the Show Place. Vince led the way, Liddell followed, prodded from time to time by the snout of Allie's .45. Inside, there was a roulette table; some slots lined the far wall, a few blackjack setups were scattered around the floor and two large dice tables were at either end. A mechanic, working on the slots, cast an incurious glance at Liddell as the two gunmen herded him toward a door beyond the far craps table.

"What's the matter? One of them pay off?" Liddell wanted to know.

Allie's answer was a particularly vicious poke with the .45. Liddell grunted, the smile faded from his face. "That iron's beginning to bug me, Allie."

"It'll do more than bug you. It'll blast you wide open, you figure you can come around here and push people around." They reached the door, Allie motioned for Liddell to stop. "Get the hands back here where I can see them," he snapped.

Liddell clasped his wrists behind him.

"See if he's heavy," Allie told Vince.

The bigger man patted Liddell down, shook his head. "Nothing."

"What do you think I am?" Liddell wanted to know. "You think I come on a social call heeled? If this wasn't a social call, I wouldn't have asked so polite to see Nast. I would have blasted my way in."

Allie snorted, jabbed the .45 in Liddell's kidney again. Johnny winced, then as Vince pushed open the door to the office, Liddell lashed backwards with his heel, caught the little gunman between the arch and the ankle. Before Allie could squeal his pain, Liddell whirled, caught him in an armlock and heaved. Allie's feet left the ground, he flew through the air, smashed into the big desk that dominated the room and collapsed in a heap on the floor.

The man sitting behind the desk was fat, soft looking. He sat there, the tips of his fingers touching across his belly, dimples where his knuckles should have been. He regarded Liddell from under heavily veined, discolored lids, seemed in no way perturbed by his entrance. His eyes rolled toward Vince, who was struggling with a gun in his shoulder holster.

"Put the gun away, Vince." The fat man's voice was heavy, sounded choked. When he talked bubbles formed and broke in the center of his mouth. The disklike eyes rolled back to Liddell.

"Johnny Liddell! It's been a long time."

"Not long enough, Harry," Liddell told him. He kicked the door shut behind him, walked over and picked up the .45 that had fallen from Allie's hand. He weighed it in his palm, nodded. "Nice iron." He slid it across the desk to the fat man. Behind him, he could hear rather than see Vince relaxing.

"You were pretty rough with my boy Allie," the fat man told him. "Allie's not going to like you, Liddell." He picked up the .45, caressed it. "He mightn't wait for you to come calling again. He might just take it into his head to go looking you up." The eyes rolled up from the gun to Liddell's face.

"Better tell him not to start reading any continued stories, then." Liddell pulled a chair close to the desk.

On the floor, Allie was groaning his way back to consciousness. No one appeared to notice.

"A friend of yours got hit today, Harry. Character named Trellis."

The fat man spat. "No friend. No loss." He sucked his lips in, puffed them out. "Why come all the way over to tell me about it? I read the newspapers."

"Trellis was scared of you," Liddell told him. "I don't think the cops know that yet." He pulled his cigarettes from his pocket, shook one loose. "When they do, they're going to come looking for you to ask a few questions."

"You're going to tell them?"

Liddell got the cigarette going, blew a stream of smoke at the ceiling. "Not unless you killed him."

The fat man snorted. "Ridiculous." He contemplated the need for motion, decided it was inevitable, reached for his bottom drawer. He pulled out a metal box, set it on the table. From his top drawer he brought a small key ring, took his time about opening the box. From it he took out a small packet of papers. "He was in me for almost $12,000. With him dead, it's not worth twelve cents." He tossed the papers across the desk, settled back. "Me, I hate welshers. But not enough to fix it so's I can never collect my money." He settled back in his chair, the lids almost obscuring the eyes.

Liddell picked up the IOUs, riffled through them.

He failed to see Allie pull himself to his feet. The thin man made a stab for the gun that lay in front of Harry Nast. He grabbed it, whirled on Liddell.

Allie's face was pale, the thin line of his mouth set, the carefully combed hair hanging down over his eyes. A thin trickle of blood ran from the corner of his mouth.

"I told you I'd blast you," he snarled. As his finger whitened on the trigger, there was a whish, a sharp crack, a scream of pain. It all happened so fast Liddell almost missed the sight of the riding crop in the fat man's hand, the speed with which he brought it down on Allie's wrist. The gunman collapsed in a chair, bent over, moaning softly.

"Take him out of here," Nast told Vince.

The big man walked over, caught Allie under the arms and helped him to his feet. He staggered to the door and they disappeared through it.

"Not that I object to what he was going to do—in principle. It's just that in practice it would have been rather awkward. There'll be other times, other places," the fat man told him smoothly.

"In that case, I won't bother to thank you." Liddell tossed the IOUs back to the fat man, who frowned at them, finally returned them to the box. "You never tried to collect these?"

The fat man's thick lips parted in a smile. "You underestimate me, my dear fellow. Of course, I've tried to collect." He laced his fingers across his mid-section. "We've had several talks with Mr. Trellis."

"Lately?"

Nast shrugged. "It hasn't been necessary. Arrangements were being made." He managed to look sad. "Now, of course, it's too late."

"How do you mean?"

"Trellis was going to work out his debt. He was going to open his act at the Show Place." He watched Liddell's reaction. "For two or three weeks, he could have filled the place. You've heard his voice?"

Liddell shook his head.

"Gone. Completely gone. For a few weeks the curious would come to see him. But that's all we needed to get our dough back. A few weeks."

Liddell got up, crushed out his cigarette. "Then you didn't kill him?"

"Afraid not, my boy. Not that I haven't considered it in the past. But right now—it wouldn't be good business. You can understand that." The heavy lids completely blacked out the disklike eyes. He appeared to have gone to sleep.

"Mind if I make a call?" Liddell asked.

The fat man moved his shoulders in an upward shrug that engulfed his chins. He continued to sit with his eyes closed, bubbles forming and breaking between his lips.

Liddell dialed the number of his answering service.

"Johnny Liddell's office," a metallic voice informed him.

"This is Liddell. Anything?"

There was a pause, then, "A Bill Nagel called. Said you knew him."

Liddell grunted, wondered what Herlehy's driver wanted.

"Said to tell you that a mutual friend had been fingered at the Hotel Sherwood and had been picked up. Said there'd be no announcement until tomorrow and that you might like to know."

Liddell swore under his breath. "Thanks." He slammed the phone down so hard the heavy lids rolled back from the fat man's eyes. He watched as Liddell stamped out of the room, slammed the door behind him, then grinned and permitted the heavily veined lids to veil the eyes again.

Inspector Herlehy sat behind the huge, unpainted desk that faced the door of his office, regarded Johnny Liddell unsympathetically. His white hair showed signs of having been raked by his fingers, a faint white stubble was beginning to glisten along his jaw-line.

"I don't owe you the time of day," he said flatly. "You knew where she was holed out. You probably stashed her there."

Liddell shook his head. "Wrong both times, Inspector. I didn't know where she was when I talked to you at Dave Trellis's place. And I had nothing to do with her going underground."

Herlehy got up, walked over to where the ancient water cooler stood humming to itself against the far wall. "Doesn't make any difference now. We've got her. Dead to rights."

"She didn't kill Trellis, Inspector," Liddell told him.

Herlehy drained the paper cup of water, crushed it and threw it at the waste basket. "No?" He flat-footed it back to his desk, picked a Thermofax copy out of his basket, shoved it at Liddell. "A letter, signed by the Mallon girl, threatening to kill him if he tossed her over." He walked around the desk, sank into his chair. "No accounting for tastes, is there?"

Liddell glanced at the letter, pushed it back on the desk. "Part of the publicity setup. Marty Lewis can vouch for that."

The inspector bobbed his head. "Already has. Also has identified the gun he gave her." He saw the look of surprise on Liddell's face. "Oh, you didn't know we found the gun? It was at her place. Under some stuff in her bureau drawer. One shot fired."

Liddell snorted. "That's crazy. You mean she knocked the creep off, went home to her place, put the gun there for you to find and then went into hiding?"

"Give us credit for something, Johnny. We know the press agent called her at her place when he found the body. He told her to get lost. She got so rattled she forgot about the gun." The white-haired man found a pack of gum in his drawer, selected a stick, denuded it of its wrapper. "The D.A. thinks we can make it stick."

"Well, I don't." Liddell got up, paced the small office. "How'd you find her?"

Herlehy stuck the gum between his teeth, chomped on it. "Some public-spirited citizen at the hotel. Said he recognized the girl and had heard we were looking for you."

"I don't suppose he gave you a name?"

"Why should he?"

"Maybe to get a medal, the lousy stool pigeon."

Herlehy grinned. "Look, I understand how you feel. It's real choice stuff and it's not going to do you even a little bit of good locked away. But that's the way the cookie crumbles, lover."

"You want to bet?" Liddell started for the door, stopped and whirled around. "By the way, where'd you get that letter she was supposed to have sent him?"

"I was wondering when you'd come to that. The letter was in her drawer with the gun." Herlehy paused dramatically, gave the wad a beating with his powerful jaws. "It had been mailed last night and was stamped received at his hotel this morning. The only way she could have gotten it was to take it off his body." As Liddell started for the door, "Where are you going?"

"I'm going to pick up the real killer for you and save you from making a damn fool of yourself." Liddell slammed the door behind him. Herlehy leaned back in his chair and grinned.

The Artists and Models Club was a converted old brownstone on the north side of East 68th Street. A canopy that showed signs of having waged a losing battle with wind and rain extended to the curb. The doorman wasn't on duty yet as Johnny Liddell drove up to the curb, paid off his cab. He walked up the short flight of stairs, pushed into the small foyer that had been converted into an entry with a coat room off to the right. Beyond, the walls to the rooms of the first floor had been knocked out to make room for a large dining area. The second floor had been similarly converted into a night club room that operated from 10 until long after legal closing.

Liddell headed for the small self-service elevator in the rear, pushed the button marked *3*.

The cage wheezed and jerked to a stop at the third floor, the doors swung open with a clang. This floor had been converted into a suite of offices. The biggest, facing on 68th Street, was marked *Private*.

As Liddell headed for the private office, Marty Lewis looked up from his desk in one of the other offices, recognized the detective. He bustled past the ante-room where his assistant was clipping notices from the evening papers, caught Liddell by the arm just as he was about to push open the door to Bunty Carter's private office.

"Johnny, what are you doing?" The press agent tried to pull him away.

"You know they got Kitty?" Liddell growled.

Lewis bobbed his head. His hand streaked for the balled handkerchief. "We did what we could, Johnny. Maybe the broad did blow her stack and burn him. Maybe he took the gag seriously and came on too big and she panicked. Could happen." His eyes beseeched Liddell's face. "No?"

"No." Liddell shook him off, turned the knob to the private office, pushed the door open.

Bunty Carter was going over a pile of reports on his desk. A look of annoyance corrugated his brow as he looked up. "What do you want?" His eyes hopscotched from Liddell to Lewis and back. "You know better than to break in here, Marty."

The handkerchief was busy again on Lewis's streaming face. "I tried to stop him, Bunty. He pushed me off."

Carter's eyes fixed on Liddell. "Okay, shamus. Speak your piece. Then get to hell out of here."

"Dave Trellis is dead—"

Bunty Carter snorted. "He better be. They're fixing to bury him."

"Very funny. But they're also fixing to burn Kitty Mallon."

"I hope you like your meat well done."

Liddell walked around the desk. He caught the night club man by the lapels, lifted him bodily from his chair. "I didn't come by to exchange bad jokes," he snarled. He set Carter down on his feet. The night club man barely came up to his chin, made up in breadth what he lacked in height. "I came by to pick up the killer."

Behind him, Marty Lewis was dancing in agitation.

"Johnny, cut it out. Bunty, I tell you, I didn't know he was coming or—"

Carter ignored him. He straightened his lapels, brushed them off. "You think I killed the creep? You must be nuts," he sneered at Liddell. "I get a yen to do a little target practice, I got better targets than Trellis. You, for instance."

"He walked out on you. After all the dough you sank in him. He was set to open at Harry Nast's Show Place."

"So?"

"So you tried to make him stay, threatened him and—"

"You're nuts." Carter opened his top drawer, pulled out a draft of an ad. "This was prepared on Monday. Three days ago. It announces our next attraction is Laurie Sands—not Dave Trellis. I knew all about his deal with Nast." He nodded his head at Marty Lewis. "Ask the flack. I gave him the office to start plugging Sands. So he had a deal with Trellis, that was his business. But he still works for me, and—"

"Bunty's right," Marty Lewis shrilled. "He—"

Liddell turned around. His right hand descended in a short arc, connected with the press agent's face, knocked him to his knees. "You little rat!"

"What are you? Crazy?" Lewis shrilled. "Bunty, make him—"

"I knew when I came here that Bunty didn't kill Trellis. You did."

The thin man's eyes rolled wildly. "He's blown his stack, Bunty. Why would I kill Dave?"

"Because after all the time and work and money you put in building him up, he was walking out on you."

"Walking out where? So he wasn't going to work our club. So, if he worked the Show Place—"

"He'd be working to pay off his paper. No money. And you knew that he'd never make another dime. So you didn't stand a chance of getting yours. You got in an argument this morning, he started to cuff you around and you blasted him."

Lewis started shrinking even deeper into his heavy-shouldered jacket. "You're crazy. Just because your broad is in a spot—"

"You got her out of the apartment so you could plant the gun and the letter. Then you fingered her for Herlehy. Didn't you?" Liddell advanced threateningly on the little man.

Suddenly from the depths of his jacket, Lewis produced a gun. "You should have pinned it on somebody else, Johnny. I wasn't sure the setup on the girl would work, but I figured you'd come up with somebody. Bunty or Harry Nast or somebody."

"Why, you little—" Bunty Carter started toward the press agent. Lewis whirled, the gun in his hand belched orange flame. The slug caught the night club man in the side, slammed him back against the desk.

Before Lewis could swing the gun on him, Liddell was on top of him. He kicked at the hand holding it, the press agent screamed his pain as the gun sailed across the room. Liddell pulled him to his feet, slammed him on the side of the jaw, knocked him sprawling across the leather library chair.

Liddell was pulling him to his feet, when the door opened.

"Hold it, Johnny."

Bill Nagel, Inspector Herlehy's driver stood in the doorway, two men from Homicide behind him.

"After all, we do want him in shape to be able to sign that confession." He nodded to his two companions who walked over, caught Lewis by the arms and dragged him toward the door.

"How come you're making like the U. S. Marines?" Liddell growled. "I thought your boss had his pigeon."

Nagel shook his head. He walked over to the phone, dialed operator. "This is a police call. Send an ambulance to the Artists and Models Club on East 68th. Sergeant Nagel, Homicide." He dropped the receiver on its hook. "Herlehy never was satisfied with the girl. It was all too pat. He figured it was a frame. And there was only one guy who knew enough to set the frame. Marty Lewis." He dug a cigarette from his pocket. "We couldn't shake it out of him. We have to go by the book." He touched a match to the cigarette. "So the inspector figured maybe we could persuade you to soften him up for us first."

Johnny Liddell sat on the couch in Kitty Mallon's apartment, drained his glass, set it down on the coffee table. The door to the bathroom opened, the redhead came out, drying her hair with a towel. She had a thin dressing gown wrapped around her. It stuck to the dampness of her body in a way that guaranteed she wore nothing under it.

She sank onto the couch alongside him, finished toweling off her damp hair. "I had to have a hot bath. You'll never know how dirty that Woman's Detention Home makes you feel."

"Probably not," Liddell conceded.

"I didn't think I'd ever feel clean again. But I do now." She swung her legs up onto the couch, cradled her head in his lap. She caught his tie, pulled his mouth down against hers. "You'll never know how grateful I am for what you did, Johnny," she told him when they broke.

He got a pretty good idea.

Dead Wrong

It was a three-story walk-up. By the time Johnny Liddell knocked on the door to 3D, he was panting heavily. It was just as well—he would have anyway the minute the door opened.

She was tall, with coppery red hair framing a heart-shaped face. A light-blue dressing gown did a half-hearted job of containing a breathtaking façade. She was high-breasted and the way the sway of her torso traced designs on the dressing gown, it was apparent she wore little, if anything, underneath it. Her trim, small waist and high-set hips gave some hint of the long, shapely legs the gown did manage to cover.

"Johnny Liddell?" Her voice was low, caressing. She studied him from slanted green eyes, from under expertly tinted lids. Her lips were full, moist.

"What's left of him." He looked back down the stairwell. "That's quite a defense gadget you've got there. More effective than a chastity belt."

The redhead grinned again, stepped aside. "But not as permanent." She took his hat, tossed it at a table. "Sit down, I'll make you a drink."

He tottered to a chair, dropped into it.

"Any preference?"

"In liquor? Scotch."

She turned, headed for the kitchen. He watched the easy play of her hips against the clinging fabric of the gown, started to feel better. When she returned, the effect from the front was equally revitalizing. She carried a bottle, two glasses and some ice on a tray, set them down on the coffee table in front of him. The devastating dip of the front of her gown as she set the tray down completed his cure, so that the Scotch would not have been needed.

He watched while she tilted the bottle over each of the glasses, dropped in a couple of pieces of ice. She picked up his glass, swirled the liquor over the ice, handed it to him.

"Mr. Liddell—"

"Johnny."

She smiled, shrugged. "All right—Johnny. When I called your office, did my name mean anything to you?"

Liddell pursed his lips, considered, shook his head. "You said Horton. Sally Horton."

She nodded, dropped down on the couch alongside him. "My husband is Bob Horton, the jazz pianist at the Nest. You've heard of him?"

Liddell nodded. "I'm not what you'd call an aficionado, but I've heard of him."

"You dig jazz?"

"I'm an old schmaltz man from away back. Carolina moon, June, spoon. That kind of stuff." He took a deep swallow from his glass. "Wasn't there some kind of an accident or something? Your husband's brother—"

The redhead turned the full power of the green eyes on him. "It wasn't an accident. Jack was murdered." She dropped her eyes, stared down into her glass. "Bob murdered him, Johnny."

Liddell grunted. He dug into his pocket, came up with a battered pack of cigarettes, held it out to the girl. She took one, stuck it between her lips. He scratched a match, waited until she had filled her lungs with smoke, then flipped one into the corner of his mouth. He lit his cigarette, exhaled twin streams from his nostrils, waited for the girl to talk.

"I suppose you wonder why I called you, instead of going to the police?" She looked up at him, let the smoke dribble from between half parted lips. "They wouldn't believe me. They think it was a hit-and-run accident."

"What makes you think it wasn't?"

"Bob and his brother haven't been getting along lately. Bob's gotten himself into debt over his head. He tried to get the money to square himself from his brother, but Jack wouldn't bail him out. The last time it happened he said he was through."

"It's happened before? Where'd the money go?"

The redhead took a deep swallow from her glass, set it down on the coffee table. "Bob has a monkey on his back, Johnny. A great big one. And it costs more than he can afford to keep it. He's been desperate for money. I heard the row the night Jack turned him down. It was pretty rugged."

"And now?"

Sally Horton shrugged. "Bob is the sole beneficiary under an old will Jack had. And there's plenty of insurance." She dropped her eyes to her lap. "I guess you're wondering why I'd be turning my own husband in like this?"

Liddell nodded. "The thought had occurred to me."

She met his gaze. "Another thing that Bob and Jack were fighting about was me. Jack and I were planning to be married as soon as I could get a divorce from Bob."

Liddell whistled soundlessly. "And you haven't told this to the police?"

"I want to be sure, Johnny. It stacks up pretty bad against Bob, but if there's just one chance in a thousand that it was an accident, I wouldn't want it on my conscience that I set him up."

"What do you want me to do?"

The soft lips set in a hard line. "On the other hand, if he killed Jack, I don't want him to get away with it. I want you to find out for me. What I do will depend on what you find."

"Where do I find your husband?

The redhead shrugged. "Any one of a half dozen pads in the Village. Almost every night at the Nest he cuts out with some of the real cool set and the blast goes until it's time for him to show back at the Nest."

She picked up her glass, drained it and held it out to him. While he was spilling Scotch over the ice cubes she said, "That won't be until about ten." She held her glass to her lips, studied him over the rim. "You'll have almost four hours to kill."

"It's going to take me almost that long to recover from that climb." Liddell reached over, helped himself to some more Scotch. "What'll you be doing in the meantime?"

"Helping you to recover."

He grinned, touched her glass with his. "That could make the collapse permanent."

The Nest was a large subterranean room that had been built by knocking out the walls of three adjoining cellars. It was lighted only by candles stuck in the necks of wine bottles, and a perpetual cloud of slowly stirring smoke swirled near the ceiling.

Mobiles dangled in the smoky air, and the customers enjoyed the proceedings from canvas chairs, while waitresses with long dank hair and dangling earrings worked their way through the chairs, their swaying hips brushing lightly against the customers.

Johnny Liddell walked down the short flight of steps from the street level, stood in the doorway looking around. He squinted into the dimness, satisfied himself that the piano on the small dais at the far end of the room was unoccupied. In another corner of the room, a tall, shaggy type in black beret and shapeless slacks and sport shirt was reading some German verse with almost comic gestures. Sitting at his feet, a bearded man was pounding unmelodiously on a pair of bongos.

Suddenly, one of the girls at a nearby table jumped to her feet, started to weave and sway in zombie-like fashion, with no expression and less grace. Nobody paid any attention.

Liddell wandered in, felt his way to a canvas chair near the wall. In a moment, one of the long-haired hostesses materialized in the dusk.

"Bob Horton going to show tonight?" he asked.

The waitress bobbed her head. "Sure thing, Pops."

"I hear he's pretty good."

"Good? He's away out. I dig him the most, man. The most. You for refreshment or just for the kicks, Pops?"

"Got any Scotch?"

The girl shook her head with no show of enthusiasm. "Chianti. Or beer." She brushed some stray hairs from her face. "You're too far downtown for Twenty-one, man. Which? Chianti or beer?"

"Beer."

The girl bobbed her head, turned, worked her way through the close-set chairs. Her jeans were easily two sizes too small.

Liddell settled back, watched the gyrations of the girl dancing to the bongo beat. He became aware of a girl sitting to his left who seemed to find him interesting. Unlike most of the wild hairdos in the place, she sported a pert gamin cut, affected a cigarette holder tilted from the corner of her mouth. When he turned to return her gaze, she grinned at him.

"Slumming, Pops?"

He grinned back. "I heard about Bob Horton. They tell me he's the swingingest. I had to hear for myself."

The girl picked up her chair, moved it over to where Liddell sat. The man she had been sitting with gave them both a disinterested look, shrugged. He turned to the girl on his other side.

She looked at the other man as though she'd never seen him before. "I been with him since last night, man. When you're making it with a cat, why that's great. But you can't stick around forever, man. You want kicks, you got to keep moving. You dig?"

"I dig." He waited while the waitress opened a bottle of beer, set it on the floor next to his chair, shoved a folded bill at her. "You like a beer or a chianti?" he asked the girl sitting next to him.

She held up the cigarette holder. "I'm swinging.

Real crazy." She watched while he poured some beer
into his glass. "You get your kicks from that? That's
real square, Pops. Try Pall Mall"—she indicated the
reefer. "It's real wild."

A broad-shouldered man with a shock of black hair
accentuating the pallor of his complexion, walked in
the front door, headed toward a door set next to the
dais on which the piano stood.

"There's Horton," the girl told him dreamily. "I
dig him, Pops. I really dig him the most."

"What's back there? Behind that door?"

The girl with the gamin cut seemed to be having
trouble focusing her eyes on Liddell's face. "He pads
down there between blasts." She eyed him curiously.
"I'm beginning to think maybe I don't dig you, Pops.
You're not here for kicks, are you?"

"Matter of fact, I came to see Horton—not to hear
him." He set his glass down by the side of his chair.
"Whereabouts is this pad of his back there?"

"Look Pops, I dig Horton. When he starts sending,
man, I get so high I know everything. I mean, like I
know why." She shook her head. "But Horton can be
a mean cat, Pops. Oh, man, you don't want to inter-
fere with him with his kick. I mean, man, what a
drag."

"Real violent type, huh?"

The girl stared down at her cigarette, a glassiness
was beginning to come into her eyes. "For kicks, Dad,
anything. He's away out. Away out."

Liddell pulled himself out of the canvas chair,
started to feel his way through the closely packed
chairs toward the door in the rear. By the time he'd
reached the door, the girl with the gamin cut had
moved in on another man, seemed to forget Liddell
had ever existed.

The other side of the door led to a damp-smelling
passageway. There was a door on either side of the
short passage. Liddell walked up to one, put his ear
to it, listened. He could hear nothing but his own

breathing. He reached down, turned the knob, pushed it open. It was stacked high with junk, appeared to be a catch-all for the buildings above whose cellar space the Nest had pre-empted.

He walked to the other door, knocked. After a moment, the door opened. Bob Horton was a few inches shorter than Liddell, but he made up in breadth what he lacked in height. His face, though, was sallow, had a yellowish tinge. His hair showed the effects of having been raked by his fingers. He eyed Liddell hostilely.

"Yeah?"

"My name's Liddell, Horton. I'm investigating your brother's death."

The man inside the door made an attempt at a sneer, didn't quite make it come off. "He's dead, isn't he? So what's to investigate?" He started to close the door.

Liddell put his shoulder to the door, sent the other man reeling back into the room. Horton recovered with amazing speed, moved in on Liddell. He threw a high left to the head which Johnny fielded with the side of his arm, took a glancing blow to the side of the jaw. It was too high to do much damage. But Liddell didn't get out of the way of a looping uppercut in time. He was slammed back into the wall, and slid to a sitting position on the floor.

He scrambled to his feet in time to handle the other man's rush to end the fight. His first left caught Horton on the side of the head, spun him halfway around. As Horton tried to right himself, Liddell buried a right in his midsection, then slammed his left against the side of the pianist's head as he jackknifed. Horton spun around, fell forward, knocked over a chair as he hit the floor. He struggled to rise, slumped back on his face.

Liddell caught him under the arms, dragged him to the unmade bed, dumped him onto it. He reached down, caught the cuff of Horton's sleeve, rolled back the sleeve. The entire inner surface of the arm was pitted with needle scars and small ulcers.

He righted the chair, pulled it close to the bed,

waited for the pianist to come to life. After a moment, Horton managed to sit up. He swung his legs off the bed, staggered to the small lavatory and retched.

When he came out of the lavatory, his eyes were watery, his hair hung dankly over his face. "I'll kill you for that, mister."

"You've done all the killing you're going to do, Pops," Liddell told him.

Horton's eyes narrowed. "Who sent you here? My wife?"

"Maybe." Liddell waited until the pianist had walked back to the bed, dropped onto it. "She thinks you killed your brother. She wants to be sure before she goes to the police." He watched the man on the bed, got no reaction.

Finally Horton looked up. "My brother was killed by a hit-and-runner. Why should I kill him?"

"For the insurance. Because your wife was getting ready to divorce you and marry him."

Horton fumbled through his pockets, found no cigarettes, finally picked a crumpled butt out of the ash tray near the bed. "That's crazy. Jack wouldn't marry her. And she knows it."

"You and your brother were on bad terms. He wouldn't lend you any money to feed that monkey of yours."

Horton made an involuntary motion toward his left arm, quickly dropped his hand. "Jack and I made that up. Right here in the club the night he was killed."

He lit the cigarette, took a deep drag, emptied his lungs. "He dropped down to see me, to tell me he changed his mind. He was going to lend me the money. Enough to help kick the habit. We were friends again. He was going to help me."

"Where were you when he was killed?"

Horton glared at him, dropped his eyes first. "Right here. Jack had left for home, I came back here. I was getting ready to cut out with some cats, and—"

"Nobody saw the car that killed your brother?"

"So?"

Liddell shrugged. He walked over to the far side of the room, pulled back a rough curtain. The window behind it had been painted black. "Where's that go?"

Horton shrugged. "How do I know?"

Liddell grinned glumly. "Make a guess." He unlatched the window, tugged it up. Outside was an alley. Liddell stuck his head out, looked up to the end where a short flight of steps led to the street level. He pulled his head in, closed the window.

"So what's that prove?" Horton wanted to know. "I never even knew it was there."

He got up, walked over to the lavatory, splashed some water into his face, raked his hair back out of his face with his clenched fingers.

"Look, mister, I've taken all the jazz from you I'm gonna take. You bust in here, push me around—" He shook his head. "I'm not taking it. So my wife hired you to frame me, go ahead."

He walked over to Liddell. "But you dig this, Pops. You listen real hard. The next time you break into my pad without a paper, you don't walk away from it. And it's all legal."

Liddell wondered just when Horton had taken his last shot, figured it must have been only a few minutes before he broke in and that it was now taking hold. The bigger and bigger man Horton felt himself to be, the slighter and slighter chance that he'd do any talking.

Liddell walked to the door, pulled it open. "The next time I bust in on you," he said, "I'll have the paper and some fuzz to serve it."

He slammed the door to the dressing room behind him, headed back into the club.

Inspector Herlehy sat behind the oversized, varnished desk in his office at headquarters, stared across at Johnny Liddell. The inspector's jaws were clomping methodically on the ever-present wad of gum, the color in his face was a little higher than normal.

"Now, suppose you level with me, Johnny." He picked up a typewritten note. "Lieutenant Michaelson in Accident Investigation tells me you've been asking for the file on a recent hit-and-run killing." He flipped the paper back onto the desk. "Why?"

Liddell shrugged. He removed the half-burned cigarette from the corner of his mouth, studied the glowing end. "I just wanted a look at the coroner's report. The kind of injuries, stuff like that."

"Why?"

Liddell replaced the cigarette in his mouth, squinted through the smoke that spiraled upward. "I'm not too sure he was killed by a hit-and-runner."

Herlehy leaned back in his chair, pursed his lips. "Neither are we." He permitted himself a grin at the drop of Liddell's jaw. "We're far from satisfied. But what put you on it?"

Liddell took a last drag on his cigarette, reached forward and crushed it out. "Horton's sister-in-law. She thinks her husband killed him."

The inspector raised his eyebrows. "Motive?"

"Jealousy and greed."

Herlehy considered it, bobbed his head. "Good motive." He explored the faint stubble along the side of his jaw with the tips of his fingers. "Opportunity?"

"Horton has a room behind the Nest. It opens on an alley that runs to the street. He says he left his brother in the club, went back to his room to rest." Liddell shrugged. "The way I read it, he could have cut out that window, run to the street, come up behind his brother and clobbered him. That's why I wanted to see the type of injuries."

Herlehy reached forward, pushed a button on the base of his phone. The door opened, a uniformed cop stuck his head in. "Get us a couple of coffees, will you, Ray? Regular for me, black for the shamus."

The cop grinned at Liddell, withdrew his head.

Herlehy turned back to Liddell. "You wouldn't be holding out, Liddell?"

"How?"

Herlehy shrugged. "You got a client on this, that I know. You implied it was the wife. It wouldn't be the insurance company?"

Liddell shook his head. "No, but it's an idea. Bob Horton is beneficiary. If it's an accident, he collects double. If it was a murder—"

"The insurance company saves plenty."

"And you think it was murder."

Herlehy eyed him blandly. "Who said so? I said we were looking into it." He reached into his basket, brought out a file. "When Mike told me you were snooping, I figured you might as well get it from the horse's mouth." He pushed the folder across the desk. "There's the Horton file from A.I.D. Medical report, everything."

Johnny Liddell lifted the report from the edge of the desk, flipped through it. He scowled at the medical report, looked up. "According to this, the injuries could have been sustained in a hit-and-run accident," he said. "A depressed lineal fracture of the skull that could have been caused by contact with the curb."

Herlehy nodded. "So, we've gone along with the hit-and-run verdict. Until and unless we can prove otherwise."

The door opened, and the patrolman returned with two containers of coffee. He set them down on the desk. When he'd closed the door behind him on the way out, Herlehy leaned forward, snagged one of the containers.

"This is the black." He pushed it across the desk, picked up the other container. "There was a car on that street that night, Johnny. A man walking his dog saw it come tearing down Sullivan Street just about the time of the accident."

Liddell gouged the top out of his container. "You got a make?"

The inspector shook his head. "The usual. A dark sedan—could be a Ford or a Plymouth or a Chevy—"

"—or a DeSoto or any other kind." Liddell nodded. He sipped at the coffee, burned his tongue and swore under his breath. "But there was a car? And it did come from where the body was found?"

Herlehy nodded. "There was a car."

"So why do you even question that it was a hit-and-run killing?"

The inspector picked up pencil, stirred the coffee in his container. "Because there was no dirt or mud where the body was found."

Liddell stared at him, scowled.

"There's always some dirt or mud dislodged from under the fender when a car hits somebody. Especially if it hits him hard enough to throw him against the curb to kill him." The inspector raised his coffee to his mouth, took a deep swallow. "Nothing."

"Then whoever was in that car could have witnessed the killing?" Liddell considered it, his scowl deepening. "Then why haven't they come forward? They wouldn't have to worry about getting tagged for a hit-and-run—"

Herlehy shook his head. "All they'd have to do would be to submit their car for an examination. No dents, no smashed headlights, no paint knocked off, they'd be in the clear." He took another swallow from the container. "But nobody's come forward."

"But why haven't you—?"

Herlehy cut him off with a glance. "Done something about it? We have. We've alerted the insurance company not to pay the policy off."

"I get it. The next move is up to the dead man's brother."

The inspector nodded. "And if that insurance is the motive for the murder, I don't think we'll have long to wait. And the faster the killer makes the next move, the more chance there is he'll make a mistake. That's what we're counting on. That the killer'll be stampeded into making a mistake."

Liddell nodded. "Maybe I can help stampede him."

Herlehy pursed his lips. "Some such thought had occurred to me."

The readhead in Liddell's outer office made no attempt to disguise her annoyance as he walked in.

"Don't tell me where to reach you, maestro. That might take some of the suspense out of this job." She tore a piece of paper out of the carriage of her typewriter, crumpled it into a ball and threw it at the waste basket.

"Something?" Liddell asked her mildly.

"Just a madman prowling the place for an hour or so, positive you were hiding under a desk. That is, from what little I could understand of what he was saying."

"Name of Horton?"

Pinky shrugged. "We didn't get that confidential. He just barged in here, busted into your office and went through the closets like he was going to give you an estimate on your old clothes."

She pushed a loose tendril of hair into place with the tip of one finger. "When I asked him what it was all about, he talked like a character out of Allen Ginsberg." She stared at Liddell. "Was he for real?"

Liddell nodded. "He plays a hot piano down at the Nest in the village. Away out. Crazy, chick, real wild."

The redhead groaned. "Not you, too? This keeps up, we're going to need an interpreter in here. What's with him and you?"

"He thinks I convinced the police that he killed his brother. He's apparently annoyed. The police have told the insurance company to hold off paying on his brother's accidental death policy and Horton probably has it all spent already."

"That could be annoying," Pinky agreed. "And if he—"

The door burst open, Sally Horton came in. Her eyes jumped from Liddell to the redhead and back. "Thank God you're all right, Johnny. My husband—"

"He's already been here," Liddell told her. He took her by the arm, led her to the private office. "We don't want to be disturbed, Pink," he told the girl behind the typewriter.

Pinky's eyes took inventory of the carrot top's assets. "Figures." She bobbed her head. "You should have been a C.P.A."

Liddell scowled at her, closed the private office door behind him. He guided the woman to the chair opposite the desk, walked over to where a water cooler stood against the wall, humming to itself. He filled a cup full of water, brought two extra paper cups to the desk. From his bottom drawer, he brought out a half-empty bottle of Dewar's. He spilled some Scotch into the two empty cups, softened it with water, held one out to the woman.

"Try this."

Sally Horton drained the cup, leaned her head back against the back of the chair. "It was real rugged. I've seen him in a rage before, but never like this. He went completely crazy."

"When did he find out about it?"

The green, slanted eyes studied him from under thick lashes. "You knew about it? About the insurance company refusing to pay off until an investigation could be made?"

Liddell spilled more Scotch into each of the cups. "I just heard about it from the police." He held out the cup, waited while the redhead took a swallow. "How come he didn't know it last night when I saw him at the Nest?"

Sally Horton shrugged. "It's like I told you. He sometimes doesn't come home for days. There was a letter there for him, but I didn't open it. This morning, he started worrying about what you said and he called the insurance company. They told him he'd already been notified they were withholding payment."

"He flipped?"

She nodded, rubbed the backs of her arms with the flat of her hands. "I've never seen him in such a rage. He went tearing out, yelling at the top of his voice."

"How'd you know he was coming here?"

"I didn't. From the state he was in, I knew he'd go looking for a fix. I've been hitting all the shooting galleries I ever heard of him using. A half hour ago, I bumped into a friend of his on Sixth Avenue. He said Bob was raving about getting even with you."

She got up from her chair, walked over to where he stood. "I came as soon as I could. If anything happened to you—" She slid her arms around his neck, pressed against him. "I couldn't stand it, knowing I got you into it."

The door to the outer office swung open, Pinky breezed in. She stood at the doorway, smiled brightly. "Pardon me." She started out again.

"What'd you want?" Liddell growled. He disengaged himself from Sally's clutches, walked around the desk. "Barging in here like that!"

"I wanted to know who to bill on this case." She looked over to where Sally Horton was inspecting her make-up in a compact mirror. "I didn't know you were discussing terms."

"When I'm ready to send the bill, I'll let you know," Liddell snapped. "And from now on, knock."

"Yes, sir." She turned to the door, then as an afterthought turned back, grinned at him. "But I don't think it would have done any good—"

"What wouldn't have done any good?"

"My knocking. I don't think you would have heard me if I pounded." She smiled sweetly in the direction of the redhead, made a production of closing the door after her.

"Quite a character." Sally Horton snapped the compact shut, dropped it into her bag. "I suppose you keep her around for atmosphere."

Liddell grunted. He dropped into the desk chair, picked up a pack of cigarettes from the desk, held it up to the girl. She shook her head, he stuck a cigarette in the corner of his mouth.

"Your husband got a gun?"

A frown corrugated the woman's forehead. "He didn't have when he left the apartment. He might have gotten one since. I—I don't think he'd try to tackle you without one."

Liddell touched a match to the cigarette, blew a stream of smoke at the ceiling. "How about you? If he gets the idea that you sicked me onto him—"

The redhead caught her lower lip between her teeth. "I think I can handle him. He usually listens to me no matter how high he's riding."

Liddell nodded. He pulled over his desk pad, scribbled an address on it. "Here's my home address and phone number. If he does show up and you can't handle him, don't hesitate to call."

Sally Horton took the paper, folded it, stuck it into her purse. "Does the same thing go if I get too lonely waiting?" She headed for the door, stopped with her hand on the knob. "It'd have at least one advantage. The doors probably lock on the inside." She opened the door, walked out.

After a moment, he heard the door to the corridor open and slam shut. Pinky walked to the door of the private office, leaned against the frame.

"How about it, boss? Do we bill her or charge it off to experience?" She grinned at the scowl on his face. "It may be fun, but you can't discount it at the bank."

It was almost midnight when Johnny Liddell dropped the cab in front of his apartment hotel. He rode the creaking elevator to the fifth floor, crossed to 506.

He fitted the key to the lock, pushed the door open. He reached in, snapped on the light.

There was a smash of glass, then two shots came so close together they sounded like one. Liddell saw them chew bits out of the door jamb at his head. He snapped off the light, threw himself forward on the floor, tugging at the .45 in his shoulder holster. Two more shots came from the window, whined over his head to smack dully into the far wall.

Cautiously he squirmed toward the window, his automatic poked out in front of him. He thought he saw a figure silhouetted on the outside, squeezed his trigger twice. The .45 sounded like a cannon in the confined space. He threw two more quick shots as a cover, pulled himself to his feet, ran to the window.

The fire escape was empty. He pulled up the window sash, stuck his eye to the corner. In the dimness of the yard, he saw a figure heading for the alley exit. He fired at it. The slug screeched shrilly as it ricocheted off the pavement.

The figure in the yard spun. There was a vicious spit as its hand seemed to belch orange flame. It spat twice more. Once it gouged a piece of concrete from the wall close enough to Liddell's head to sting him with its splinters. He pulled his head in. By the time he looked again, the figure had disappeared through the doorway into the alley.

Liddell scowled at the pounding on his door. He walked back, snapped on the light, tugged the door open. A white-faced manager stood in the doorway. "What's going on?" he quavered, his eyes hopscotching around the room, coming to rest on the .45 in Liddell's fist.

"Sneak thief," Liddell grunted. "No harm done."

"That's what you think," the manager complained. "Half the tenants have been scared out of a week's growth. Mrs. Maher down below had a fainting spell and—"

Liddell pushed the door closed. "Tell them it was a Civil Defense drill. Tell them the next time they hear shooting to head for the shelter." He closed the door in the man's face, headed for the telephone stand.

The directory gave the number of the Nest as We-6

2359. He slammed the book shut, dialed the number. After a moment, a shrill voice came through the receiver.

"The Nest. Good evening."

"Let me talk to Bob Horton."

There was a slight pause. "Sorry, Pops. He ain't showed yet tonight. Ain't heard a word from him. But we got some Gerry Mulligan biscuits that—"

Liddell depressed the bar on the phone, waited a few seconds, then dialed a number. He listened to it ring five times, then a sleepy voice growled at him. "This is Herlehy."

"Sorry to call you at home, Inspector."

"Who is this?"

"Liddell. Now, wait a minute—" He staved off any complaint. "I wouldn't have called if it weren't an emergency. If you want to stop another killing, you'd better pick up Bob Horton."

There was a slight pause. "Why?"

"Somebody just shot up my apartment. Horton hasn't shown at the upholstered sewer he works in. By now, the fat's in the fire. The insurance company has already served warning they're not paying off. There's no telling what he'll do next."

The sleepiness was gone from the inspector's voice. "I'll get the boys right on it. If you get anything, don't try grandstanding. Get right back to me. I'll be in my office."

"Me, grandstand? You know me, Inspector."

"Yeah. That's why I'm warning you. No grandstanding!" There was a click as the connection was broken.

Liddell dropped his receiver on its hook. He walked into the kitchen, brought in a bottle of Scotch, some ice and a glass. He poured himself a stiff shot, dropped in ice. Then he brought a box of cartridges out of the drawer, starting reloading the .45.

He was on his third cigarette and his second Scotch when the telephone shrilled at his elbow. He scooped the receiver up, held it to his ear.

"Johnny? This is Sally Horton." Her voice was low, breathless. "I'm in the lobby of your building. Can I come up?"

"Come ahead. I'm in room five hundred six."

"I'll be right up."

Liddell frowned at the receiver, dropped it back on its hook. He walked into the kitchen, brought in another glass. He had just filled it with ice and was washing it down with Scotch when there was a knock on the door. He slid the .45 from its holster, walked over to the door, pulled it open.

It was the redhead. Her eyes went wide at the sight of the .45. He grinned at her, stuck it back into its hammock. "Don't mind the artillery. I've already had a visitor this evening who antiqued my furniture with bullet holes. I wanted to make sure you were here under your own power."

Sally Horton walked in. Her eyes took in the smashed window, the fresh scars in the wall and door where bullets had gouged out deep splinters. She turned to Liddell. "Was it Bob?"

He shrugged. "Figures. He didn't show at the club tonight." He led her to the table, handed her a drink. "Whoever it was waiting for me when I got home, he was a lousy shot. But I'm not planning to give him a chance to improve with practice."

The girl took a deep swallow from the glass, set it down. Her face was scrubbed clean of make-up, save for a smear of lipstick. She wore a full-length camel's hair polo coat, loafers, no stockings.

"He's home. At my place." She caught Liddell by the lapels. "He's a crazy man, Johnny. I managed to lock myself in the bedroom and get out by the fire escape. He was raving and ranting about being double-crossed. I was scared."

"Why didn't you call me?"

"I don't want him to kill you, Johnny. And he will. I tell you he's crazy."

"Sit down and catch your breath." He helped her out

of her coat, whistled softly. Under it she wore only a pair of light-blue pajamas, the trouser legs rolled up to her knees.

"I—I was ready for bed when he came. I was too scared to take time to dress. I just grabbed a coat and ran."

Johnny fought to keep his glance at face level, lost the struggle. "I'd better get over there. You make yourself at home until—"

She caught his hand. "Don't go now. Give him an hour or so. I know Bob. He'll knock himself out, then pass out." She was close to him, he could feel her breath on his face. "I don't want anything to happen to you."

"I'd better get it over with. I'll be back."

The redhead shrugged. She walked over to the end table, helped herself to a cigarette. "Suit yourself."

When she turned and walked toward him, the sway of her torso traced patterns on the shiny silk of her pajama jacket. "Please be careful." She walked up to him, covered his mouth with hers.

Johnny Liddell stopped outside the Horton apartment, put his ear to the door. The only sound was his heavy breathing after the three-flight walk-up. He tugged the .45 loose from its holster, reached for the knob. It turned in his hand. He pushed the door open, stepped back out of range. After a moment, he stepped into the open doorway, fumbled along the wall for the switch.

Bob Horton sat in an upholstered chair not ten feet from him, staring at him with unblinking eyes. His arm dangled over the side of the chair, almost touching the .38 that lay there. A stream of red ran from the corner of his mouth. There was a small black hole through his left temple, with a ragged rip on the side of his jaw where the slug had taken a piece of the bone with it on the way out.

Liddell closed the door, walked over and stared

down at the dead man. He reached down, pulled up the sleeve on Horton's right arm. In addition to the punctures he had seen the night before, there were several new ones, discolored, angry looking, an inch or so apart.

Liddell walked to the bedroom door, tried it. It was still locked. He took a last look around the room, walked to the telephone, dialed headquarters.

"Inspector Herlehy," he told the operator.

"The inspector comes on in the morning. I'll let you have—"

Liddell persuaded the man at the switchboard to try the inspector's office, heard the grunt of surprise when Herlehy answered.

"This is Liddell, Inspector. I found Bob Horton at his place."

"Keep him there. I'll have some men—"

Liddell glanced over at the man slumped in the chair. "Won't be any trouble keeping him. He's wearing the hole from a .38 for an extra ear." He could hear the inspector's breath hiss through his teeth. "Gun's right here on the floor beside him."

"We'll be right over."

Johnny Liddell slouched in the big chair, watched the redhead bustling around his kitchen. The smell of coffee was strong and promising. Sally Horton still wore the flimsy pajamas, rolled to the knees, a shirt of Liddell's draped over her shoulders, the tails flapping ludicrously as she walked.

Even the loose shirt couldn't disguise the fluidity of her movement as she walked toward him, balancing a cup of coffee on a saucer. She made it without spilling a drop, pushed it at him triumphantly. She grinned as he tasted it, burned his tongue.

"That's an old trick," Liddell complained. "Burn my tongue so I can't taste that the toast is burned." He set the cup back on the saucer. "You'd better be thinking about going back to your place, hadn't you?"

The smile dimmed. "Must I?"

Liddell shrugged. "Herlehy will probably want to be talking to you. After the coroner's done with the autopsy."

The smile went blank, some of the color drained from the girl's face. "Autopsy? But he shot himself. You don't need an autopsy for that. You said yourself—"

"He had a bullet hole in his head. It came out through his jaw." He watched the muscles form little knots at the sides of her jaw. "A suicide rarely holds the gun so high the bullet comes out lower than at the place of entry."

She backed away from him. "Then you killed him?"

Liddell grinned glumly. "No. You did."

He took a swallow of the coffee, put cup and saucer on the floor alongside his chair. "And in a little while, Inspector Herlehy'll be able to prove it."

"You're crazy," she told him in shocked certainty. "Why should I kill my husband?"

"For one thing, because you're tired of him. You might have stuck if he could hold onto his brother's insurance. At least until you figured a way to get it away from him."

"But I hired you. I was the one who told you he killed Jack. If it hadn't been for me—"

Liddell shook his head. "The police weren't fooled. When you opened that letter from the insurance company saying they were withholding payment, you knew you had to find a patsy. And your husband was made to order."

She shook her head wordlessly, backed away. "You're wrong. Bob killed his brother. You said so yourself."

"I said that he could have. That was all part of your plan. You waited outside in the car. When Jack came out, you clouted him with something—a tire iron probably. Then you took off." He watched the girl's face. "The police have a witness to the fact that a car was in that alley when Jack was killed."

"You can't pin that on me."

Liddell sighed. "The worst part of it was that it was all for nothing. Even if the police write your husband's death off as suicide, you can't collect the money."

The color flooded back into her face. "I do. I'm his only heir. As his wife—"

"You get what he had. But if the police buy the story that he killed his brother, he can't collect either the insurance or the estate. There's a little clause in the law that says a murderer can't benefit from the fruits of his crime."

The color started to drain away again. She stared at him. "I—I killed for nothing? I—I couldn't collect anyhow?" Her eyes began to glaze as she started to laugh. Her laughter hit a high peak, she began to shake uncontrollably.

Liddell got out of his chair, shook her. She continued to shrill. He hit her with the flat of his hand; the laughter broke off on a high note. She stared at him.

"I hated him but I would have stayed for the money. Now I get neither." She looked up at Liddell. "What do I do, Johnny?"

He shook his head. "That's up to you, chickie. But whatever you decide to do, you'd better do it fast." He consulted his watch. "That autopsy ought to be over in an hour and they'll have all the proof they need that Horton had been fed a skin full of junk and then shot."

The redhead stared at him. "How could you know?"

"There were two real fresh punctures on his arm. One was enough to send him out of this world—the other to keep him there. And the autopsy will show it." He watched while she walked over, shrugged into her coat. "Where are you going?"

"To give myself up." She smiled at him wanly. "I can't wait to see whether I killed him in a moment of temporary insanity or in self-defense. Watch the papers." She walked to the door, left.

Liddell reached down, picked up the cup and saucer.

He stared glumly at the coffee, pulled himself out of the chair and spilled the coffee into the sink. He lifted the Scotch bottle from the closet, spilled three fingers into a glass.

"What a waste of good material," he groaned.

He lifted the glass to his lips, drained it, shook his head sadly. "What a waste!"

Dead End

Johnny Liddell stared at the girl who lay stretched out before him. Her hair was ash blond, almost wheat-colored. Her eyes, showing under half-closed lids, were blue, complemented by the faint blue tinge under them. Her lips were full, sensuously shaped, her teeth small and white.

She was uncovered to the waist, her small, perfectly molded breasts exposed to the yellow light.

She wasn't much over twenty, he estimated, and the ominous blue coloring around her mouth and lower cheeks made it pretty certain she wouldn't get any older.

He waited while Inspector Herlehy of Homicide pulled the rubber sheet up over her face. The white-haired man dug a wadded handkerchief from his hip pocket, swabbed at his forehead.

"Died from a hot shot—overdose of morphine," he he said. "Doors locked from the inside. Verdict posted is suicide." He nodded toward the small office that adjoined the examining room. "Let's go inside."

He turned, his heels beating a noisy tattoo on the cement floor as he led the way into the next room. It was furnished with a metal enameled desk, some filing cabinets and two chairs. The inspector hoisted one hip on the corner of the desk, waited until Liddell had closed the door after him.

"Well?"

Liddell shook his head. "An awful waste of good material. But where do I fit in? I never saw the kid before in my life."

"I know." Herlehy took off his fedora, and laid it

on the desk. He raked his fingers through his hair. "Her name is Jackie Wells. Comes from a small town upstate. We're shipping her home tomorrow. As a suicide."

"But you don't think she was?"

Herlehy shook his head. "She gave herself the hot shot, all right. She was into something over her head and I guess this looked like a good way out." He dug into his breast pocket, brought out an envelope, passed it over to Johnny Liddell.

The private detective dumped out a batch of four-by-five prints, flipped through them, whistled noiselessly. "Pretty raw." He returned the pictures to the envelope, and handed it back to Herlehy.

"Obviously she was mixed up in the dirty pictures racket," he said. "That's where you come in."

Liddell shook his head. "Thanks for the compliment, Inspector. But I take a terrible picture."

The white-haired man ignored the interruption. "She may have killed herself, Johnny. But the guys behind this racket"—he tapped the envelope—"set her up for the kill. Her and who knows how many other kids."

Liddell dug a battered pack of cigarettes from his pocket, held it out to the inspector, drew a shake of the head. He selected one himself, stuck it in the corner of his mouth, waited.

"I talked to that kid's father on the phone. I had to break the news to him." Herlehy scowled. "She was a good kid. Stagestruck, maybe. But a good kid. That was less than a year ago. Now she's a suicide, a hophead and"—he held up the envelope—"this. I want the men who made her that way, Johnny. And I think you're the man who can get them."

"You got eighteen thousand men wearing a badge who could—"

"They've got other things on their mind—more than they can handle, Johnny. Sure, they're working on cleaning up the dirty pictures racket, but just as part of their job. I want somebody who can give it his full time—make it his hobby as well as his job." He squinted at Liddell. "There's not much money in it. But a lot of kids like that one would be awful grateful. So would I."

Liddell took the cigarette from between his lips, rolled it between his thumb and forefinger, stared at it thoughtfully. "How far do I go?"

"I don't want to know. But don't bring them in just for taking dirty pictures. The most they can get that way is sixty days. If that's all you can get on them—don't bring them in at all. Just make them wish you had."

Liddell grinned, stuck the cigarette back in his mouth, squinted through the smoke. "I'll do what I can, Inspector. Anything more that will help me? Where she lived, stuff like that?"

Herlehy got off the corner of the desk, walked around it. Wordlessly he opened the top drawer, lifted out a manila envelope, passed it across the desk to Liddell. After the private detective had left, the white-haired man raked his fingers irritably through his hair, swore under his breath.

Jackie Wells had lived in an old brownstone building that nestled anonymously in a row of identical brownstones in the East Seventies. Johnny Liddell left the cab at the curb, walked up the short flight of steps to the vestibule.

Inside it was cool, damp. The hallway smelled musty, spiced with the smells of ancient cooking and inadequate toilet facilities. Her apartment was first floor rear. He walked the length of the dim hall, fitted her key to the lock, pushed open the door.

The living room showed signs of police activity. A chalked outline on the floor next to the sagging sofa showed where the body had been found. Liddell checked the doors leading off the living room. One opened on a small bathroom, the other led to a bedroom that looked out on a small backyard. An unmade

bed revealed gray linen, and some articles of clothing were draped over the back of a chair. There was
no evidence that the room had been searched in any
way.

Liddell walked over to the rickety bureau that was
topped by a fly-specked mirror, tugged at the top
drawer.

He stiffened at the sound of a key in the lock outside. He slipped the .45 from its shoulder holster,
edged up to the door opening on the bedroom, and
put his eye to the crack.

The hall door swung open. A tall redhead walked in,
closed and locked the door behind her. She was staring
at the chalked outline on the floor when Liddell
stepped into the living room.

Her eyes widened at the sight of the gun in his hand,
her fist shot toward her mouth. "Who are you?" she
managed to croak.

Liddell slid the .45 back into its holster. "Sorry to
startle you. I thought I had the only key to the place.
I'm a private detective. Name's Johnny Liddell. I'm
looking into Jackie Wells's death." He saw the girl's
brow furrow with puzzlement. "Just to satisfy the
family."

The redhead's brow cleared. "Oh. She did commit
suicide, you know."

Liddell nodded. "I've already checked that out with
the police. As I said I'm just doing a routine walk-
through for the family." He let his eyes take admiring
inventory of the redhead's long-legged, full-breasted
frame. "And you?"

"Sandy Roberts. Jackie was a good friend. I was
going to gather up any of her personal belongings her
people might like to have."

Liddell looked around the apartment, scowled. "Any
idea of what kind of a jam she was in?" he asked.

The girl considered, shook her head. "She didn't talk
much." She walked over to the sagging couch, dropped
onto it, crossed long, shapely legs. "I never met any of

her other friends—men or women."

Liddell looked at the legs. "Where'd you meet her?"

"We attended the same modeling school. We both dropped out about three months ago. Since then I haven't seen her as often as I used to." She shrugged. "But I figured the least I could do was gather her things together for her folks."

"Why'd you drop out?"

The redhead shrugged. "It's just my opinion, but I thought it was a fake. They'd promise you everything —and never deliver. I can't afford to throw my money away like that."

"Where is this place?"

"What are you going to do?"

Liddell shrugged. "I'm not sure yet. But if it is a gyp, I'm going to get Jackie's money back for her folks."

"It calls itself New York School of Glamour. It's in the Graybar Building. A woman named Joy Marvin runs it."

"Where can I find you in case I happen to get your money back, too?"

The redhead hesitated for a moment, then grinned at him. "I live in the Hotel Sentinel on Forty-eighth Street. But I won't hold my breath until you get my money back from Joy Marvin."

In New York, the Graybar Building sits cheek to jowl with Grand Central Station and stares glumly at the Chrysler building towering many stories above it from across Lexington Avenue.

Johnny Liddell found the suite number of the New York School of Glamour, walked to the bank of elevators and rode up to the 18th floor. Double glass doors at the end of the hall announced the school. A single row of small gilt letters in the corner of the right-hand door read: *Joy Marvin, Directress.*

The ante-room was filled with girls in all sizes and all shades of hair. At their feet stood the ever-present hat-box identifying their profession. A telephone operator-receptionist sat in a glass booth that faced out on the ante-room. She was leafing through the pages of a movie magazine and seemed undisturbed by the hum of conversation, which was spiked by the occasional occurrence of high-pitched laughter.

Johnny Liddell walked to the glassed-in cubicle, rapped on the window with his knuckles. The girl inside managed to look annoyed, slid back the panel.

"Yes?"

Liddell dug a little leather folder from his pocket, flipped it open to reveal a shield. "I want to see Joy Marvin." Some of the conversation had dribbled away into silence. The girls looked from him to each other.

The receptionist's eyes flashed from the badge to Liddell's face and back. She nodded, slid the panel shut, stuck a plug in a hole and wiggled a key back and forth. While she spoke into the mouthpiece, her eyes never left Liddell's face. She yanked the plug out, slid the partition back. "She'll see you now, officer."

An electric latch stuttered, and a door to the right of the glassed-in switchboard opened. Liddell walked through. The corridor beyond was lined with small offices. At the end of the hall, a woman stood in the doorway of a double office. She watched him impassively as he walked down to where she stood.

When he reached the door, she turned and walked back to her desk chair. The effect from the rear was good, and when she turned to face him, Liddell found the flip side equally interesting. She must have been thirty-five, but her face had the texture and smoothness of a much younger woman. Her hair was platinum-white, complemented by the deep tan of her skin. Her eyes were slightly slanted, the effect enhanced by careful make-up, the mouth a red slash in the cocoa color of her skin.

She returned Liddell's scrutiny, her expression non-committal. "I understand you're here in an official capacity. May I see your credentials, Mr.—?"

"Liddell." Johnny held the leather folder toward

her so she could see the badge, started to return it to his pocket. She reached out, caught his hand.

"Not so fast, please. I haven't had time to admire your pretty shield." She examined it, nodded. "I see. You're a private detective. No official standing."

"No official standing."

"In that case, I'm afraid I'm too busy to—"

Liddell cut her off. "Of course, if you have something to hide, when I come back it might be with somebody with official standing."

The smooth brow of the platinum blonde was corrugated with an annoyed frown. "What's that mean?"

"A former pupil of yours thinks the modeling course is a fake. She hired me to get her money back."

"That's ridiculous."

Liddell shrugged. "Maybe. I thought I could save you a lot of annoyance and bad publicity if you'd cooperate. But perhaps you'd prefer to have her take it up with the License Commissioner."

The angry frown was still on the woman's face. "Who is this ex-pupil?"

"Jackie Wells."

The frown of annoyance deepened. "We never should have taken her in the first place."

"You were right. You never should have taken her, for all her money. Then when she ran out of money—"

"Mr. Liddell, this is a reputable school. Out in our ante-room are a dozen girls who work regularly. You're free to question them." She got up, walked to the filing cabinet against the wall, pulled it open. "Here are hundreds more of our graduates. Upstairs, classes are going on." She slammed the cabinet shut. "We can't bat a thousand. Jackie Wells just wasn't the type we're looking for."

"I think she was. She had money." He watched the color rise on the woman's face. "She didn't stop being the type until she ran out of it."

"If Jackie Wells told you that she's a liar."

"She didn't tell me anything. Jackie Wells is dead. A suicide."

"I'm sorry to hear that, of course." Joy Marvin walked back to the desk chair, and sat down. She reached for a cigarette, got it lit before she continued. "Jackie Wells was impatient to get where she was going. We have a certain curriculum and we insist that our girls be completely trained before they accept jobs." She shrugged. "Jackie wanted to accept assignments before we thought she was fitted for it."

She removed the cigarette from between her lips, studied the carmined end. "She's not the first girl who refused to submit to the discipline we consider necessary in a model. And she won't be the last."

"These girls in the outside office. What kind of jobs are they waiting around for?"

"Fashion modeling, photographic modeling."

"Nudes?"

Joy Marvin reached over, crushed out her cigarette with icy calmness. When she looked up, her eyes were flashing with repressed anger. "I think I've taken all the insinuations I'll take from you, Liddell. You come in here representing yourself to be a policeman."

"No official standing. You said so yourself."

"But you imply we're running a crooked school and that we rent our girls out for immoral purposes." She pulled the phone over to her. "That last one was just a little too much. This is a respectable business. And we're entitled to police protection."

"Why don't you call the police?" he challenged.

To his discomfort, she did.

Inspector Herlehy sat behind his desk, ran the tips of his fingers along the bristle glistening on his jowls. He studied Johnny Liddell, slumped in the chair across the desk, with no show of enthusiasm.

"Sure, I want you to find whoever's behind the dirty pictures racket. But I didn't tell you to go busting into a respectable model agency and start throwing muscle around. You've got to use some discretion, Johnny."

He picked up a flimsy, shook it at Liddell. "She screamed so loud I had all I could do to keep the Commissioner from lifting that potsy you're so proud of flashing. I had to perjure my immortal soul to convince him how many times you've gone out on a limb to co-operate with the department."

Liddell growled deep in his chest. "Just the same, it's the ideal setup. A talent or a modeling school gets hold of these stagestruck kids and provides them for stag movies or pornographic stuff. I'll bet that."

"Well, don't. All you've got is a hunch, and that Joy Marvin is within her rights screaming persecution. You stay away from there. You got that?"

"You claim you want me to find whoever's behind the ring. Then when I start feeling my way, you lower the boom."

"Not me. The commissioner," Herlehy reminded him. "Besides you're going about it backwards. Find the creeps who are using the girls and they'll lead you to whoever's providing them."

He got up, and walked over to where an old water cooler stood against the wall, humming to itself. "I'm not saying you're wrong about the Marvin dame's setup. But until you can prove what you think—stay away from her."

He filled a paper cup with water, drank it and crushed the cup in his fist. "I promised the commissioner you would. He made me a promise, too. He said if you went near Marvin again, he'd personally pull your ticket off your office wall." He threw the balled cup at the waste basket.

"I still think the Marvin school's behind it." Liddell held up his hands to ward off another torrent from Herlehy. "But I won't go back there until I can prove it. Okay?" He pulled himself out of his chair, walked to the door, stopped with his hand on the knob. "And when I do go back, I'll be the one who yells copper.

Not her!" He slammed the door after him.

That evening, Johnny Liddell leaned against the bar in the Club Cubanola, shifted his jigger to his left hand, turned around and peered into the smoky opaqueness of the cocktail lounge beyond. Overhead a blue-gray pall moved sluggishly near the ceiling. Down the bar, a white shirted bartender was assuaging his boredom by polishing the mahogany with a desultory semicircular motion that left greasy circles.

Liddell grunted his satisfaction when a well-stacked brunette walked into the cocktail lounge, and headed for a table in the rear. He drained his glass, set it back on the bar. He fumbled through his pockets, came up with a hand full of change, dumped it alongside the glass.

The girl was just touching a match to her cigarette when he walked up to the table, pulled out a chair, slid in across from her. Her eyes widened, her lips twisted in a pleased smile.

"Johnny Liddell! Where'd you come from?"

"I've been trying to reach you. But I couldn't break through that answering service of yours." He reached for her pack of cigarettes, spilled one out and stuck it between his lips. "I need some help."

"And here I was, thinking maybe you were getting ready to break down and come calling sociable like." The girl shook her head. "What's the matter with me, Johnny? Not your type?" She held her cigarette up, let him light his from it. "Any night you decide to come calling, that's the night the shop is closed. You know that, don't you?"

"I'll be around, Katie."

She opened her bag, brought out a small memo book, scribbled a name and a telephone number on the top sheet. "The answering service bit is strictly for Johns. You ever want me, you call this number and I'll come running." She tore off the sheet, passed it to him.

Liddell took the penciled memo, studied it and nodded. He put in into his pocket. "You know most of what's going on in town, Katie. How about the dirty picture boys? Who's making them these days?"

The dark-haired girl dabbed at an ash tray with the end of her cigarette, shook her head. "It's not operating like in the old days, Johnny. Used to be a couple of the girls in the life would have tough sledding, their old men would set up a picture date at some studio and they'd split even on the take."

She returned the cigarette to her lips, winced as the smoke stung her eyes. "It's been organized lately. They're using amateurs and chippies. None of the regulars will work for the mob that's running it now."

"Why not?"

Katie shrugged. "They play rough, for one thing. They set up a swinging party and use hidden cameras. Like that, they not only get pix, but they're in the business of selling home movies and home recordings at the same time."

"Who's they?"

The dark-haired girl took a deep drag on her cigarette. "I don't look good with black eyes. It clashes with my hair."

"Bad boys, huh?"

She shrugged again. "Bad enough, from what I hear. They're giving the girls a run for their money. For a price, they'll deliver anything from a dowager to a deb. And they've got enforcers to make the delivery stick."

She tapped a thin collar of ash from the cigarette. "That's why there hasn't been a peep. Most of the girls mixed up with them are semi-legit and have too much to lose by squawking. And a John who'd be too careful to get put on the spot with a pro, gets real careless with a café society chick. The mob's taking it from both ends."

"And you don't know who I should have a talk with?"

"I don't want to know, Johnny. And unless it's real worthwhile, I don't think you ought to go sticking your nose in, either." She grinned at him. "I'm a lot less dangerous. And I'm available. And the price is right. With you, it's strictly amateur night."

"As soon as I get this wrapped up, I might just take you up on that."

"Make sure it's the case, and not you that gets wrapped up. These boys aren't going to appreciate somebody ruining their racket." She took a drag on her cigarette, crushed it out in the ash tray as a waiter walked up to the table. He eyed Liddell questioningly.

"It's okay, Paul. Liddell's a friend."

The waiter bobbed his head in acknowledgment. "It's a telephone call, Katie. Your service."

The dark-haired girl made a face, smiled at Liddell, got up and followed the waiter to the bar. She gave her hips a little extra twirl for Liddell's benefit—he got the message.

When she returned, she shrugged. "An important one, Johnny. Runs away from the old woman twice a year and comes to spend a week in New York. I see him almost every night when he's here." She picked up her gloves, started to slip her fingers into them. "I'd even pass him up, if—"

"I can't, chickie. Not until I've finished what I've started." He crushed out his cigarette, stood up. "You dig?"

"I dig." She tapped his arm, started for the door, turned and walked back to him. "Put me in a cab, Johnny?"

He caught her elbow, piloted her through the tables. At the curb, he waited until the uniformed doorman had whistled down a cruiser. The cabby zoomed in, banged his front wheels against the curb, drew a dirty look from the doorman. He ignored him, studied Katie appreciatively as she got in.

"If you're really set on what you're after, Johnny," she told him through the open glass, "look up a man named Barney Grant. I think he might be your answer."

She winked at him, turned to the driver, gave him an address and then sank back against the cushions.

Liddell stood at the curb, watched the driver fit his cab into the stream of traffic, take the first right on two wheels. He turned the name Barney Grant over in his mind several times. It struck no familiar note.

The BCI—the Bureau of Criminal Identification—is located on the first floor at Police Headquarters. It's known as the Gallery to the working cops who use its facilities, as the Rogues Gallery to the public whose only contact with it is in television plays. It's the *Who's Who of Crime* and anyone who has ever passed through the hands of the law has left his pedigree there.

Johnny Liddell leaned on the counter that split the room in two, watched the uniformed clerk checking through his files. Finally, the clerk looked toward Johnny, shook his head.

"No Barney Grant." He indicated the Oddities File and the Nickname File. "Got anything we can use for a make in Oddities or Nickname?"

Liddell shook his head. "Just that. Barney Grant."

"Sorry, Johnny," the uniformed man told him. "We have no package on a Barney Grant. Not under that name. How about the MO file?"

Liddell shrugged. "It could be worth a try."

A huge chart on the wall breaks down all the sixty-two varieties of crime encountered by the department alphabetically—ranging from arson to worthless checks. Each crime is further broken down into subdivisions and alongside each is the number of the file in which known operators in that category are listed.

Pornography specialists were listed in Files M and N. These files contained thousands of records and pictures of men who have been either indicted or convicted of making, selling or processing pornographic material. It took only a few minutes to determine that no Barney Grant was listed.

Liddell waved his thanks to the man behind the partition, headed out into the lobby.

For the rest of the afternoon, Johnny Liddell kept on the move. He started at 50th and 8th, hit most of the news-stands and taverns on the side streets off Broadway. He only stayed a few minutes in each place. But when he left, the operator or the man behind the bar knew he was looking for information—and was willing to pay. It could be risky. The wrong ears might hear about it. But the chances were even stronger that the right ears would hear about it.

He was back in his office across from Byrant Park by nine. He sat at the open window, his heels hooked on the sill, fingers laced at the back of his head, and stared out at the red outline of the Enna Jettick sign across the park on 40th Street. Its hands pointed to 10:15 when the phone rang. He lifted the receiver carefully. A reedy voice came through the earphone.

"Liddell? Ain't seen you around in a long time. Been wondering how you been doing." There was a pause, then the whine of the stoolie's voice was back. "This is Willie Morse."

"I'm fine, Willie. Something on your mind?"

The whine was more pronounced. "You been good to me, Liddell. I figured I owed it to you to say good-by."

"You going some place, Willie?"

"Yeah. An ex-con don't stand a chance in this town. I been thinking of blowing it. So I figure I'd like to say good-by. Face to face. You know?"

"Drop by any time."

There was a slight pause. "That mightn't be a good idea. Some people see me going into your office, they might get the idea I was shopping information. That mightn't be a good idea."

"Maybe I could meet you someplace."

"That'd be real nice of you, Liddell. You wouldn't be sorry."

"Where?"

"I got a pad on Eighth near Forty-ninth. Tonight

maybe around twelve I'll be out front. Drive past real
slow. If everything's all right, I'll wave you down."

"I'll be there." Liddell dropped the receiver on its
hook, stared at it for a moment. It could be a dry run,
but Willie sounded scared enough to have something
worthwhile.

There are all kinds of stool pigeons who live on the
fringe of New York's seedier side. Some are legit, operators of places where criminals aren't welcome. Some
stool to get rid of a rival, or to get revenge. Some just
stool to prove how much they know and about whom.

But there's another group—the Little Men. These
are men like Willie. Small-timers who may be thrown
a bone by the Big Shots, who run their errands and
take their abuse. Willie was a Little Man.

He carried a monkey on his back, an addiction that
dated back to a series of painful operations following
a flash fire in a tenement years before. The monkey
got bigger as the years passed and Willie's petty little
rackets didn't pay enough to keep its appetite satisfied.
Willie was not an informer for any of the usual reasons. Willie was an informer because he found that
people would pay for what he knew. And as his monkey grew in size, Willie found more and more items
to sell. Sometimes the information was valueless, more
often it was worth far more than it cost. Liddell had
learned from experience to take it when it was offered.

At 12:05, Johnny Liddell drove north along Eighth,
hugging the curb as he approached 49th Street. It still
showed signs of life although the Garden up ahead
was in complete darkness, even its marquee lights
doused. A few drunks wove down the street. Some sat
on steps, their heads sunk below their knees; others
snored in doorways and vestibules. None of them both-
ered the occasional groups of sailors, their arms an-
chored around half-drunken floozies as they staggered
to their mooring for the night.

The car had reached the corner of 49th when Liddell
spotted the little man standing in the shadows of a

darkened store front. He braked to a stop; Willie Morse shuffled across the sidewalk. He was short and fat, his head kept swiveling from side to side as he hustled toward the car.

"Evening, Liddell." He looked around as Johnny opened the rear door, slid into the back seat and flattened himself on the cushion. "Mind if we keep moving?" Willie mopped at his face. "I wouldn't want for anybody to see me riding with you."

The car jumped into motion, Liddell headed for Central Park.

"What do you hear around that's interesting, Willie?"

The stoolie twisted his loose lips into a semblance of a smile, shrugged. "Things have been pretty bad, Liddell. The Man cut off my credit. I been shooting cotton for a week already." He wiped at his mouth with his sleeve. "I don't like to ask for a handout but tonight I hear you're making a buy."

"If it's what I want."

The man in the back seat pursed his lips, his Adam's apple bobbed nervously. "It'd have to be worthwhile. I'd have to get out of town."

"How much, Willie?"

Willie twitched nervously. "A hundred?"

Liddell looked into the rear-view mirror. "Sure it's not to get you off the hook with the Man to buy you a couple of caps?"

"Honest, Liddell. I'm going to kick the habit. No kidding."

"This information. What is it?"

"Dirty pictures. Movies and stills. That what you want?"

Liddell nodded, piloted the car around a slow moving sedan, headed into the park. Willie straightened up on the back seat, made a futile, mechanical gesture to smooth the wrinkles out of his suit.

"It's a new mob operating. They got it fixed so nobody can yell copper. They work it on guys who can afford to pay, but can't afford the publicity. The come-on is all fresh stuff. Young kids, amateurs." The whine was back in his voice. "That worth a hundred?"

"Maybe. The name Barney Grant mean anything to you?"

Willie licked at his lips. "Look, Liddell. I don't want any misery. You got to cover me."

"You want the hundred, don't you? What you've given me is worth about ten dollars worth. What do you know about Barney Grant?"

"It's no name. It's a password." He put his hand on Liddell's shoulder. "You won't spill you got it from me, will you?"

"Have I ever? What's it a password to?"

"I don't ask questions. All I hear is a new outfit is running a shakedown racket on out-of-town Johns." Willie reached up, swabbed at the streaming sweat on both sides of his jowls. "They keep a pad in the Hotel Breen on Forty-seventh Street." He swabbed at the streaming jowls again. "You figure that's worth the hundred?"

Liddell reached into his pocket, brought out a roll of bills. With his thumb he separated the top bill, a century note, held it back over his shoulder. Willie grabbed it, checked the denomination against the window.

"Where'll I drop you?"

"First exit on the Eighth Avenue side." Willie looked out the window of the car, tried to decide where they were. "You'll be real careful Liddell, won't you? I mean about where you got the tip. I hear these cats are real mean and I wouldn't want them coming to look up old Willie."

Liddell swung the car to the left, pulled up at the side of the road. "You can get out here. Cut through the bushes and you're at Eighth Avenue." He watched the fat man struggling to get out of the back seat. "Remember, you were going to use that money to kick the habit."

Willie managed to get through the door. "I mean it, Liddell. This time I'm really going to kick it. You'll see." He headed into the shadow of the bushes, melted into the darkness.

He waited there until Liddell had the car in motion and the tail light blinked around the nearest turn. Then, hunching his shoulders and digging his clenched fists into his pocket, he started shuffling in the direction of Eighth Avenue. The subway would take him to where the Man had his regular stand. The hundred would cover the twenty he owed the Man and provide a good supply of caps for a couple of days. After that? Well—he'd worry about that then.

The Breen Hotel was an old, run-down building on the north side of 47th between Broadway and Sixth. A small plaque to the right of the door dispelled any doubt as to its character by announcing it as the Hotel Breen.

A threadbare and faded rug ran the length of a lobby that had long since given up any pretense of serving a useful purpose. The chairs were rickety and unsafe, the artificial rubber plants grimed with dust.

Johnny Liddell ignored the old man behind the desk who raised rheumy eyes as the private detective passed, then dropped them back to a perusal of the scratch sheet spread out in front of him. Liddell made directly for the lone elevator cage in the rear. A pimpled youth with slack mouth and discolored eyes stared at him apathetically as he stepped into the elevator.

"Barney Grant," Liddell told him.

The slack mouth twisted into a wet smear of a grin. The operator winked one eye obscenely, slammed the elevator shut. "Sixth. Must be a real swinger tonight." He watched the floors crawl by the open grille work of the door. "It sounds like a gasser."

The elevator ground to a spine-shattering stop, Pimple Face slammed the door open. "It's room six-oh-six." He nodded his head to a door at the end of the hall, stood in the doorway of his cage, watched Liddell until he reached the door.

A narrow-chested man with thick, wavy hair opened the door in response to Liddell's knock. "Must be the wrong room, mister. This is a private party."

"Funny. Barney Grant told me to drop by. Said there'd be some laughs and stuff." Liddell snaked a ten-spot from his pocket, folded it between his fingers.

"Friend of Barney's, eh? That's different." The narrow-chested man brought his right hand out of his pocket, clamped it damply around Liddell's. When it was withdrawn, the bill was gone with it. "Come on in. It's the right room now."

He stepped out of the doorway, waited until Liddell was in the outer room, closed the door behind him. From another closed door, Liddell caught snatches of muted laughter, the sounds of a party in full, hilarious progress.

"Sounds like it's beginning to jump."

"It'll get better," Narrow Chest told him. He bolted the door, led the way across the room. He opened the other door, pushed away a heavy curtain that was hung from ceiling to floor as a means of deadening the noise.

Inside, a radio phonograph combination was grinding out a frenzied rhythm beat while half a dozen or more couples danced, pasted closely against each other. The chairs and sofa had been pushed back against the wall to make more space for dancing. Thick, oily smoke swirled lazily around the one indirect light in the room, filling the air with a sickish sweet aroma.

The narrow-chested man left him at the door. Liddell wandered through the man-made fog toward an open door that apparently led to the third room of the suite. The room beyond was bathed in a dull blue light. There was no furniture in the room, but a dozen or more men and women were draped on cushions scattered around the floor.

A tall blonde danced wildly in the middle of the

floor, her hair flying, her body undulating and throbbing. As Liddell watched, her motions become more and more abandoned until suddenly, with a wild scream, she ripped at her clothing, tore it from her and threw herself into the arms of a man draped on a small pile of pillows.

As if that were the signal, the other couples became more and more indiscreet in their love making. As Liddell's eyes became accustomed to the gloom, he could see that several of the girls had already divested themselves of their clothing.

A tap on his arm caused Liddell to spin, his hand automatically going for his right lapel. The narrow-chested man stood behind him.

"You didn't have a girl, mister, so—"

Behind Narrow Chest stood Sandy Roberts, the redhead Johnny had met in Jackie Wells's apartment. The girl's eyes widened as she recognized him. Narrow Chest's eyes hopscotched from the redhead to Liddell and back.

"What's wrong?" he snapped.

"You jerk! How'd he get in here? He's a private detective."

Narrow Chest's jaw sagged. He made a swift recovery, started to shout a warning. Liddell's right traveled only a few inches, buried itself in the thin man's midsection. The air wheezed out of his lungs like a punctured balloon. Before he could straighten up, Liddell caught him on the side of the jaw, sent him sprawling back into the room.

The private detective had the sensation that the dancers had frozen in a pose of suspended animation. They stood watching him.

Sandy backed away, screamed. "Joe! Eddie! It's the law!"

The dancers, standing with frozen, shocked expressions seemed to come to life. In a moment chaos broke out in the room. Men and women rushed for the door. The crowd from the darkened room almost knocked

Liddell over as they rushed through. Then, as suddenly as it started, it was over. The room was empty except for the unconscious man on the floor.

Liddell tugged the .45 from its holster, walked into the dimly lit room. He looked around, a mirror on the inside wall caught his attention. He walked over, examined it. It was a two-way glass, and it covered a small opening that had been drilled into the room—an opening large enough to permit the panning of a camera from the adjoining room.

He rushed for the outer room. Narrow Chest was just beginning to groan his way back to consciousness. Liddell pulled a pair of cuffs from his pocket, handcuffed the semiconscious man to the radiator.

"In case you get the wanderlust, you can take the plumbing with you," he grunted.

He pushed aside the sound-deadening drape, crossed the outer room to the hall. The door to the adjoining suite was unlocked. He turned the knob, pushed it open, stepped to the side, flattened himself against the wall, waited. There was no sound from inside the room—the only sound was of heavy breathing. His own.

Gun in hand, he ducked into the room, sank to his knee alongside the door as he pulled it closed.

There was a smash of glass, then two shots came so close together they sounded like one. Liddell could see them chew pieces out of the wall above his head. Splinters and plaster stung his face. He aimed at the only light fixture in the room, blasted it off the wall, throwing the room into darkness.

The man on the fire escape blasted again.

Liddell aimed at the spot where the orange flash had been, squeezed the trigger twice. The .45 sounded like a cannon in the confined space. There was a scream from outside the window, a dim shape stood outlined on the fire escape.

Liddell squeezed the trigger again. The man on the landing shuddered under the impact of the heavy slug, staggered backwards. The low railing caught him off balance. For a moment his arms flailed wildly. Then he disappeared and the landing was empty.

Somewhere a woman screamed. The scream seemed to hang on the air, then cut out suddenly.

Liddell felt his way across the room to a bridge lamp near the far wall. He snapped it on, spilled yellow light into the room, walked to the window and threw the sash up. A group of men were huddled around a dark bundle in the courtyard below. He pulled his head in, walked over to the wall that connected the room with the suite beyond.

A small stand had been set under the hole in the wall that was covered with the two-way mirror in the other room. He examined the infrared camera that was used to record the orgies in the dark, swore under his breath.

Then he walked to the phone, dialed headquarters. The door to the suite burst open, the slack-lipped elevator operator stuck his head in, looked around. He stared at Liddell.

"My God. You're bleeding!"

"You ought to see the other guy," Liddell grunted. He turned back to the phone. "Inspector Herlehy in Homicide," he told the headquarters operator.

Joy Marvin, directress of the New York School of Glamour, sat in the wooden chair opposite Inspector Herlehy's desk, accepted a cigarette from Johnny Liddell. The cocoa-colored face was gray, looked drained of all color, leaving her lipstick and eye-shadow as dark smears against the pallor.

"This could ruin me, Inspector," she told the white-haired man behind the desk. "It could look as if—"

Herlehy shrugged. "The dead man did work for you, Miss Marvin. There's no doubt many of the girls used by the ring were recruited from your school."

"But without my knowledge. How could I know that Stiles approached these girls, offered them short cuts to modeling and movie careers?"

There was a knock on the door, a uniformed police-woman ushered the redheaded Sandy Roberts into the room. She looked around, dropped her eyes when she recognized the woman in the chair.

"You know Miss Marvin, Sandy?" Herlehy wanted to know.

The redhead hesitated, then nodded. "I know her."

"Stiles worked for Miss Marvin. You knew that?"

"That's where I met him. When I was taking her course." She looked up at the white-haired woman defiantly. "He was crazy about me right from the start. We were going to make a killing so we could go some place away from her and start over. She never left him alone. She was after him to—"

"That's a lie," the woman in the chair got to her feet, tried to twist out of Liddell's hands when he restrained her. "She's the one who put the idea into his head!"

"He couldn't stand you," Sandy taunted. "He only stayed with you because he needed bread. A couple more months of this operation and he wouldn't need you any more. You or your money!"

Liddell pushed the white-haired woman back into her chair. "What about Jackie, Sandy?"

The redhead shrugged. "One of those things. She got on Horse, kept going down. Stiles got her to work with us by telling her he was shooting some love scenes that would be used in European versions of pictures. When she found out what she was in, she kicked at first—" She shrugged. "She went along."

Herlehy made a face as if he had swallowed something sour. He pulled the envelope of stag shots from his desk, waved them at the redhead. "Maybe these helped keep her in line."

"You can't prove anything by me, Inspector."

"Maybe not. But we can show you the inside for a couple of months. And at that you're lucky. The only thing Stiles will see the inside of is a box."

The redhead tried to meet his glare, dropped her eyes first.

"Get her out of here and see that she's booked for attempted extortion, Sergeant."

He waited until the policewoman had led Sandy from the room, before he turned to Joy Marvin. "I don't think we need you any more, Miss Marvin."

"My name won't enter into this in any way?"

Herlehy considered, shook his head. "Not this time. But take a cop's advice. Be a little bit more careful— a little more careful in choosing your men and a little more careful in taking care of the girls you're supposed to be training."

An angry flush colored the woman's face. She started to retort, instead got out of the chair, left the room without a backward glance.

Herlehy got up and opened the window.

"Okay to make a phone call, Inspector?" Liddell asked.

"Go ahead. You're entitled to some fee."

"I wanted to call Katie Rawson."

The inspector turned, stared. "Rawson? She's a—"

Liddell nodded, started dialing. "She's a pro." He looked up. "I don't think my stomach could take much more of these amateurs."

The Killing

Marty Riker had damp, dreamy eyes. The sleepy eyes, combined with an esthetic pallor, a long face and pouty lips, gave Marty Riker an appearance of being far removed from the baser facts of life. In some circles he was called the Poet because of his predilection for what the other members of his set considered the classics. He had even once been observed carrying a volume of Shakespeare, although those in the know were aware that in those days, as a runner for Charley the Book, he had used the pages of the Bard to carry the day's selections from the other books who had laid off on Charley.

Although the days when he affected a long, flowing hair-do were comfortably in the past along with his activities as a runner, Marty still liked the better things —fast horses, fast women and fast profits. But he only liked them if they belonged to him.

Mendy Waltz sat in the tastefully furnished apartment-office from which the Poet conducted most of his affairs and watched with thinly disguised apprehension as Marty pursed his lips and scowled at the list of figures before him. He covered the growing dampness of his palms by fumbling through his pockets for a cigarette and lighter.

Finally the Poet leaned back, his eyes rolled to the ceiling, he touched the tips of his fingers across his chest. "The third time in a row we take a shellacking on that Witt entry." His voice was soft, carefully modulated. "It couldn't be the guy's a brother-in-law, Mendel."

Mendy worked at a nonchalant shrug, didn't quite

make it. "We can't win them all, Marty. Look at the other tracks. We make a killing every place but here. So we write it off your income tax."

A look of distaste crossed Riker's face. "You'll please leave my income taxes out of the discussion. When I'll need advice on what I should leave out of my income tax, you I won't come to. For this I pay Spec plenty." His eyes rolled down from the ceiling, fixèd themselves on Mendy. "To you I come when I see red on the day's tally." He leaned forward, picked up the column of figures, fixed a hurt glance upon the total. "Every time it's the same. The Witt Stables got an entry, I got more red on my tally than the local blood bank."

Mendy smoked with short nervous puffs, his mind fumbling for any straw to get him off the hook. "So from now on you lay off on the Witt entry. Maybe Joe Garry in Chi or the Bug in L. A. will take it. By the time they get wise to—"

"This is real smart advice"—the Poet nodded, his dreamy eyes reproachful—"real smart. This way, instead of losing money, I lose my best outside man. You." He flipped the tally back onto the desk. "You know what happens to a wise guy who pulls a fast one on the Bug?" He shook his head. "Real smart advice."

Mendy managed to look abashed. "Yeah, Marty, I wasn't thinking so good. This Witt business got me real upset, too. Real upset." He wrinkled his forehead to give unmistakable evidence of how hard he was thinking. "If something would only happen to Old Man Witt—"

"This you didn't tell me," Marty chided. "I thought it was his horses beating us. The old man is running?"

"You know what I mean, Marty. Something happens to his stable or his horses." He watched the Poet's face, warmed up to the subject. "Nothing permanent, you understand, just something so we make a real killing. Get back what he's been costing us."

Riker pursed his lips thoughtfully, massaged the tips

of his fingers along his hairless chin line. "Sort of at the last minute, you mean?"

"Yeah, yeah. Right at the last minute. Like that we make a real killing." He crushed out his cigarette, leaned forward. "You know the old man. He's got rocks in his head. Even if his horse had a broken leg, he'd run his entry. Something happens to his Blue Queen, he ain't got a dog can run the whole distance, let alone win a race."

Marty Riker picked up the tally sheet again, looked ill at the splash of red at the bottom, nodded. "It might work. But remember, Mendel. Me, I know from nothing. Somebody goofs, we're going to miss you around here."

But Mendel was beyond caution, carried away with the brilliance of his idea. "Who could goof? Look, we'll take every layoff on the Witt entry we can lay our hands on. The boys all know that with you it's a jinx. We can make a killing."

The Poet's eyes were dreamy, his pale face seemed at peace. "Sure. One way or another, a killing!"

2

Connie Witt was a throwback to the early days of racing when a man, two horses and a schedule of county fairs constituted a way of life. He had been following the horses for over fifty years and now, in the twilight of his career, he had achieved his lifetime ambition. He had his own stable—three horses—and he had been upsetting the experts at tracks all over the country. True, two of the horses would have been more at home in front of a milk wagon, but with Blue Queen he had what every track man dreams of, a horse that was all heart, mounted on four of the fastest legs in the game.

Johnny Liddell leaned on the rail at the exercise track, watched the big horse thunder down the stretch, pound past the marker. He looked over to the owner, grinned at the scowl of concentration on Connie's face.

"What's the matter, Cornelius? What's she doing, dogging it? She didn't even break the track record that time."

"Don't call me Cornelius," the old man growled. He shoved the battered, sweat-stained fedora on the back of his head, stroked the silvery bristles along the side of his jaw. "She come within seconds of that time, she's got it sewed up, Johnny." He looked up, watched while an undersized Negro in riding breeches, a maroon turtle-neck sweater and reversed baseball cap walked the big horse over to where they stood.

"How'd she handle, Rufe?" the old man wanted to know.

The boy showed white teeth in a pleased grin. "She just took that one easy, Mister Connie. She eats this track up." The smile faded a little. "She do all right in time?"

The old man winked. "All right, boy. Real all right."

The lustre returned to the big-toothed smile. "Yes, sir, I sure thought so." He patted the horse along the side of the muzzle. "Come along, Madam Queen, we'll get you rubbed down nice and dry." He led the horse past in the direction of the stables.

"How about her stablemates, Connie?" Liddell asked.

The old man spat a dun-colored stream of tobacco at the track. "Don't expect much from them, Liddell. The Queen's a temperamental old girl. Don't like running a damn, unless she has one of her mates running with her. Doesn't matter whether they last or not, she runs her heart out when she knows they're in there with her." He pulled a plug of tobacco from his pocket, bit off a chunk. "I don't know if you remember her or not, but Silver Queen, the Blue's stablemate—she's out of the same mare by the same stud."

"Blood relatives, eh?"

"Let's go over, make sure they're walking out the Blue." He caught Liddell by the arm, started in the direction of the stables. "Silver Queen was the big money horse in the stable when the old Colonel was alive." He shook his head. "Even better than the Blue."

"What happened?"

Connie pulled the old fedora off his bald head, scratched the startling whiteness of his pate. "Broke a small bone couple years ago. We should have destroyed her maybe, or just used her for breeding, but the Colonel loved having her around." He replaced the hat on the back of his head. "When he died, he left the stable to me and I made up my mind—as long as I'm racing, Silver Queen wears the stable's colors."

"You run them as a stable entry, eh? If I want to get a couple of bucks down on the big race next week, I just bet the entry. Right?"

The old man winked. "You bet that entry, son. The old Blue'll leave them all behind." He looked around and dropped his voice. "And that crook Marty Riker'll be going to the cleaners when she does."

Liddell nodded. "I gather you've been costing the Poet a lot of money this season. Word's around the Witt Stables is his jinx."

"A lot of people like the Queen, Johnny, and they're people whose business Riker can't turn down. They'll be doubling up on this one to really take him. I never bet on horses, but I'm putting every dime I can scrape up on the Queen. She's a breeze."

3

The exercise boy was just finishing walking the big roan around the compound when Connie and Liddell walked up. The old man's face split into a broad grin when he saw the Olds convertible parked near the stable. A tall, slim girl with short red hair waved from behind the wheel.

"Hi, Connie."

"It's Miss Elsie, the Colonel's kid, Johnny. Come on over and meet her." He started toward the car in a slow lope, let Liddell follow after.

From close up, the girl looked older. Wind and sun had given her face a creamy tan which blended with the copper color of her hair. Her eyes were deep blue, engagingly direct. She wore no make-up but a slash of scarlet lipstick. A green cashmere sweater paid tribute to the lushness of her figure.

Connie was already pumping her hand when Liddell walked up. "You sure are a sight for sore eyes, Miss Elsie. It's been a long time since you came around to see us."

"Since Dad died, Connie." Her voice was sultry, throaty. She made no attempt to hide the interest in her eyes as she looked Liddell over.

"Oh, this is Johnny Liddell, Miss Elsie. Or maybe you know him?"

The redhead shook her head. "I've heard of Mr. Liddell." Her eyes took in the thick shoulders, the thick hair flecked with gray, the square chin, the humorous eyes. "I didn't know you were a jockey, Mr. Liddell."

Liddell grinned. "Just a track buff, Miss Elsie. I like to come down and get my information from the horse's mouth. That way, when I lose I have someone to blame it on."

"Don't you believe him, Miss Elsie," the old man interrupted. "I asked him to drop by." He looked around and dropped his voice. "The word's out that the Poet—"

"The Poet?" the girl wanted to know.

"Marty Riker, a big-time bookie we've been taking for plenty," Connie explained. "Word's out he'll cover anything and everything against the entry."

Elsie looked worried. "Maybe he knows something about one of the other horses that makes him so sure."

Connie shook his head. "Nothing I don't know better. I just clocked the Blue and she's lengths better than anything in the field." He scratched at his chin. "The Poet knows that, too. He could win only if something happened to the Blue."

"He wouldn't hurt the horse?"

The old man showed yellowed teeth in a grim smile. "He'd cripple his own mother if he could make a buck doing it. I'm not so much worried about losing the race as I am that something might happen to the Blue—"

Liddell clapped him on the shoulder. "Don't worry about it, Connie. Nothing's going to happen to Blue Queen. You keep clocking her at that time and she's in." He turned to the carrot top. "It's been nice meeting you, Miss Elsie. Connie, I'm afraid I've got to be getting that bus back to town."

The girl grinned at him, reached over and opened the door to the car. "I'll give you a lift. You know that's what you're hinting for."

"You talked me into it." Liddell walked around the car, slid in beside the girl. "You're sure I'm not taking you out of your way?"

Elsie winked at the old man, turned the key and revved the motor into roaring life. "Just be sure I don't take you out of yours."

4

Elsie Grant lived in a richly appointed apartment in one of the cliff dwellings surrounding Central Park. A small hallway led into a tastefully furnished living room, beyond which a sun deck seemed to be pasted to the wall. The girl led Liddell through the French doors to the deck. It had a gaily colored awning that protected it from the curious above, and walls that guaranteed it privacy from the neighbors on either side. Directly in front, and eighteen floors below, sprawled Central Park, its lake glistening like a piece of mirror in the midst of the lush green of its foliage.

"There, isn't this better than your old office?" the girl wanted to know. "It's too hot to work today." She walked to the railing, stared down into the park below. "He's a real old character, isn't he?"

Liddell dropped onto a divan set against the wall, stretched his feet out. "Any one of those dots down there in particular?"

The redhead giggled. "You know who I mean. I mean Old Connie. He's so sure his horses are unbeatable."

Liddell dug a cigarette from his pocket, stuck it in the corner of his mouth. "I don't know about his horses, but if that one I saw work out today can do that time in an actual race, she's in." He touched a match to the cigarette, exhaled smoke in twin streams through his nostrils.

The girl walked over, stood in front of him. She reached down, picked the cigarette from between his lips, took a deep drag on it. "I went out there today because I knew you were going to be there." Smoke dribbled from half-parted lips. "Pretty brazen female, eh?"

Liddell grinned up at her. "Connie tell you?"

Elsie shook her head. "I've got my sources. Don't forget the Witt Stables belonged to my father when Connie was just a trainer." She dropped down alongside Liddell on the divan. "What are you going to do for Connie?"

Liddell shrugged, retrieved his cigarette, studied the smear of carmine on the end. "I don't know if I'll have to do anything. He just wanted some advice. How to protect his horse against any possible harm."

"You going to guard the horse?"

Liddell grinned. "That's one I've never tried, body-guarding a horse. No, Connie doesn't need any help. He has enough of his own boys to take care of any emergencies."

The girl leaned back, jutted her breasts against the

soft fabric of the sweater. "This Poet, do you know him?"

"I couldn't say I'm a bosom friend, but I know Marty. He's a two-bit hustler who chiseled his way into the big money." He studied her as he smoked. "Why?"

She shrugged. "Just curious." She chewed for a moment on the tip of a well-shellacked nail. "Liddell, can I tell you something in the strictest of confidence?"

"Why not?"

"I'm in a jam." She shrugged her shoulders. "I'm beginning to see now that I was backed onto this spot, but nonetheless I'm on it." She got up, started to pace the porch. She was lithe, her well-filled sweater tapered down to a narrow waist that hinted of full hips, long, shapely legs concealed by the long sheath sport skirt. "I don't know if you knew my father?"

Liddell shook his head.

"He was a wonderful old guy, Liddell, but he had one fixation. He was death on gambling, always said that it was changing racing from a sport for gentlemen into a racket." She stopped in front of him. "One of the reasons he gave Connie the stable is because he was furious with me for gambling. It was in my blood, I couldn't help myself. He thought that by giving away the stable and keeping me off the track he'd cure me."

Liddell nodded. "But it didn't?"

"It never does. But I had to be careful. By the terms of his will, I can lose my share if I gamble. And his executor is just as death on gambling as Dad was."

Liddell lit two cigarettes, held one out to the girl. "You've gotten in deep again. To Marty?"

The girl stopped with the cigarette halfway to her lips. "How did you know?"

"It didn't take a detective to guess you were pumping me for somebody, nor a genius to figure out it was for Marty." He stared up at her. "What does he want you to do?"

The redhead raked her fingers through her hair. "He wants me to arrange for something to happen to Blue Queen. He knows that some of the old stable hands are still loyal to my father. They'd do anything for him—if I asked." She crushed the cigarette out unsmoked. "I can't do it, Liddell, I can't do it. When I heard you were going to be out there today, I thought maybe you could help me."

"How deep are you into the Poet?"

Elsie caught her lower lip between her teeth, worried it. "About twelve thousand."

"And he's pressing for it?"

"It's no great secret about the terms of my father's will, apparently. Marty threatens to go to the executor with my paper." She raised her hands palms up in a helpless gesture. "If he does, I've had it."

"How can I help you?"

"You can come with me when I tell Marty I'm backing out."

Liddell took a last drag on his cigarette, crushed it out. "If you're sure that's what you want to do."

"I've thought a lot about it, Liddell. I'm sure that's what I want to do." She stared at him for a moment, then grinned glumly. "How about a drink? I, for one, can use one."

Johnny Liddell nodded, watched the rhythmic play of her hips against the tight skirt as she walked back into the kitchen. When she returned with a tray of ice, glasses and bourbon, the view from the front was equally satisfying. She pulled over a small glass table, set the tray down on it. "You pour," she invited.

Liddell dumped a couple of ice cubes into each of the glasses, drenched it down with bourbon. He swirled the liquor around in the glasses, handed one to the girl. "You look like you think the world's come to an end," he said.

The girl flashed him a rueful smile. "You think it hasn't?"

Liddell smelled the bourbon, tasted it. It tasted the

way it smelled—top grade. He took a deep swallow. "Seems to me the big problem is to get the IOUs back from the Poet. Then you're in."

"Sure. And in the process double-cross an old friend of my father's and sell my soul down the river." She shook her head, took a deep swallow. "Things are tough, Liddell, but not that tough."

"I meant get them back—take them back."

The girl looked at him for a moment, comprehension dawning slowly in her eyes. "You mean—take them back? Just like that? Go up and take them back?"

"Why not? I'll give him my receipt for them. Then, after we win the twelve grand on Blue Queen, we give him what you owe him. In the meantime, the IOUs will be in a safe place where nobody can show them to the executor."

The girl dropped down beside him. "You'd do that, Liddell?"

He was uncomfortably conscious of her closeness, of her vitality. "Why not?"

She set her glass down. "I've always heard there were men still around, but in the circles I've been traveling I've never met one—until today." She slid her arm around his neck, found his mouth with hers. Her lips were soft, moist. After a moment, she pulled back, studied him in undisguised admiration. "Just like that—we'll go up and take them away from him." Her breath was warm, fragrant on his cheek. "He won't be up for hours." Her fingers raked through his hair. "What'll we do until then?"

"We'll think of something."

5

Marty Riker's combination office and apartment was in the penthouse of the Seaview Hotel, a huge pile of plate glass and mortar that hung over the East River in the early Fifties.

Elsie Grant turned her convertible over to the doorman, followed Johnny Liddell through the huge glass
door that led to the ornate lobby. It was furnished in
modernistic style, the thick pile of the carpeting was
almost deep enough to mow. A small reading room,
furnished with heavy leather armchairs and subdued
lighting, was to the left. A chattering neon sign announced a cocktail lounge to the right.

Johnny Liddell plowed through the heavy pile of
the carpet to the desk. A man in a morning jacket,
with just the tip of a snowy white handkerchief peep-
ing from his breast pocket, watched his approach with
cold eyes. He tugged at the cuffs that showed a rim of
white, waited.

"Mr. Riker. Will you tell him Miss Grant is here
concerning some paper."

The man behind the desk didn't alter expression.
"Go up. Mr. Riker's apartment is on the twelfth floor.
I'll tell him you're on your way."

The elevator bank was in the rear of the lobby. As
Liddell ushered the redhead into the car, a tall, tired-
looking man followed him in. The operator slammed
the door, the car started to whoosh softly upward.

"You're going to see Riker?" the tired man wanted
to know.

Liddell looked him over, nodded. "Yeah. Any objection?"

"Just a suggestion," the other man drawled. "The
piece. Leave it with me. Mr. Riker is very nervous
about guns." His eyes looked sleepy, the lids half hid
them. But the hand in the jacket pocket looked like
real business.

Liddell tugged the .45 from its holster, handed it
over. "It's a social call."

"Sure," the other man agreed. "They always are. I
make sure of it." He hefted the .45 in the palm of his
hand. "A nice piece. Use it much?"

"No. I just carry it to make my coat hang straight."

The car sighed to a stop at the 12th floor, the door

slid open. Mendy Waltz stood outside the door to Riker's apartment. He looked past Liddell to the tired man questioningly.

The man in the elevator nodded. "He's clean."

Mendy returned the nod, waited until the closing door of the elevator had blocked off the guard's face. He turned to the girl. "Who's this guy? The boss don't say nothing about holding a mass meeting. He wants to see you."

"The boss won't like your discussing his business out here in the hall either, Mendy," Liddell told him. "Suppose you let us tell him about it."

Mendy scowled at him, started to retort, shrugged. "Okay, go in." He pushed open the door, waited until they had entered the apartment, then followed them in.

Marty Riker sat behind his desk, working on his nails with a small pocket knife. "What's on your mind, Miss Grant?"

"We'll wait until you're finished if it's that important, Poet."

Riker's sad, dreamy eyes rolled up from his highly shellacked nails. "Oh, the great Mr. Liddell." He looked at Elsie with sad accusation. "I just told you to find out what he was doing, not to bring him out here."

"I'm not going through with it, Marty. You can do what you want to do with my IOUs, I'm not going through with it."

The Poet looked hurt, made a production of closing his knife and stowing it in his pocket. "That's a bad attitude. You make a deal, you stick by it. Otherwise, you get hurt, Miss Grant."

The redhead licked at her lips. "I've thought it over. I got myself in the box, I'm willing to take what's coming to me."

"Maybe it wouldn't be pretty." Riker leaned the flat of his hands on the top of the desk, lifted himself to his feet. "On your say-so, I have a lot of money invested. A lot of money that says Blue Queen don't run. It would make me very unhappy to lose all that money. I get real unpleasant when I get unhappy. Huh, Mendy?"

Mendy grunted. "Like the Poet says. A deal's a deal."

"You're scaring her to death, Poet. You wouldn't want to force her to do something she didn't want to do?"

Riker grinned a slow, sad smile. "Somebody invited you, Liddell? This is between the broad and me. You got no vote here." He snapped at Mendy. "Keep the shamus quiet."

Liddell turned, looked at Mendy who looked uncomfortable. He had tugged a snub nose .38 from his jacket pocket. He gestured with it. "You heard the boss, shamus. Keep out of it."

"You know what they teach at the FBI Academy, Mendy? They teach you never to pull a gun unless you're going to use it."

"What makes you think he won't?" Riker growled. "You think this is a penny-ante book operating out of the back of a cigar store? This is a big operation; no tin-horn shamus or no spoiled society broad is going to knock it over."

Liddell took two steps to the desk, reached across it, caught the Poet by the lapels and pulled him halfway across the desk. He moved so fast that he caught Mendel flat-footed. By the time Mendy grasped what was happening, Liddell had the Poet in front of him.

"Go ahead, Poet. Tell him to shoot."

6

Beads of perspiration glistened on the sad-faced man's forehead and upper lip. He stared at Liddell's face from under heavily lidded eyes. "I'll kill you for this. Mendy! Get the boys."

Mendy started for the door, couldn't move fast enough as Liddell threw the Poet at him. They collided, collapsed into a jumble of arms and legs. The impact knocked the gun out of Mendel's hand, sent it spinning across the floor. Elsie scrambled after it, came up with it in her hand.

"I've got the gun, Liddell," she said.

"We won't need that. This is strictly a business proposition." He walked over to where Riker and his stooge lay tangled on the floor, pulled the Poet to his feet. "Miss Grant owes you twelve grand. Right?"

Riker bared his teeth. "You can't buy them back. They're going where they'll do the most good." He flashed a venomous glance at the girl. "Maybe the double cross will cost me dough, but it'll cost you more."

Liddell took a handful of the man's shirt, pulled him up on his tiptoes. "Nobody said anything about buying them back. I'm giving you my IOU for the money in exchange. You act nice, and maybe I'll even add interest."

The Poet started to bluster, sputtered out as Liddell pulled his face closer. "I'm doing this real business-like, Poet. We don't go out of here without the paper. Whether you still have teeth or not when we go depends on how fast you get the idea."

Riker tried to meet Liddell's eyes, dropped his first. "Okay. You got the drop on me, Liddell. That's the way it's got to be, that's the way it's got to be. I had you figured too smart to stick your neck out that far for any broad."

"Never mind the conversation. The paper." He pushed Riker away, sent him stumbling backward. "Pull anything, and the only way you'll know what happens will be by ouija board."

The Poet yanked a set of keys from his pocket, walked behind the desk. He unlocked the top drawer, fumbled in it. Liddell walked over to the girl, relieved her of the gun.

"Bring the notes out with two fingers. If anything

but a pack of papers comes out, I'll blast your hand off."

Riker brought up some papers with thumb and forefinger, dropped them on the desk.

"See if they're all there, Elsie," Liddell directed.

The girl picked up the stack of IOUs, riffled through them. "They are. All of them."

"Burn them." He motioned with the gun. "In the brass ash tray." He waited while the girl touched a match to the paper, watched it curl into black ash, then crumble into gray powder. "Okay, now make out an IOU to Riker for value received and I'll sign it."

"I'll get you for this, Liddell," the Poet promised. The menace in his voice didn't seem to match the dreaminess of his eyes. "And don't think it'll do any good. Blue Queen won't win, she won't even run."

Liddell ignored him, waited until the girl had finished writing the note. He walked over to the desk, picked up the pen and signed it. "There you are, all businesslike. We just discounted your notes for you." He motioned for Mendy to join his boss behind the desk. "Just to avoid any misunderstanding, I'm going to ask both of you to step into the lavatory for a few minutes."

The Poet started to growl his objections, shrugged, led the way into the lavatory. Liddell closed the door behind them, wedged a chair under the knob.

He winked at the girl. "I told you he'd be understanding." They walked to the door, rang for the elevator. The tired-looking man was in the cage with the operator. He nodded to Liddell as he and the girl stepped in, waited until the doors had closed and the car started downward.

"Well, here's the piece." He tugged Liddell's .45 from his pocket, passed it over. "Nothing personal, you understand. Just a precaution."

Liddell grinned at him. "Sure, I understand. I'm the same way about guns. Can't stand someone else hav-

ing them." He brought Mendel's .38 from his pocket.
"Give this back to the Poet when you see him. I forgot to give it back as we walked out."

The tired-looking man's eyes widened, but he kept
his hand conspicuously away from his pocket at the
sight of the .45 Liddell still held in his hand.

"By the way, the Poet may be wanting you, so when
we get out of the elevator, don't bother getting out
with us. You'd better get right back up to see him."

7

The telephone on the table next to Liddell's bed
started to shrill. Johnny Liddell cursed softly, dug his
head into the pillow but the noise refused to go away.
He opened one eye experimentally, determined it
wasn't yet dawn. The sleep wouldn't wipe out of his
eyes, and the telephone wouldn't stop ringing, so he
snaked one hand from under the covers and lifted the
receiver off its hook.

"Yeah?"

"Johnny? Elsie Grant. Johnny, are you awake?"

Liddell growled. "I wasn't."

"Get dressed and wait for me outside your place.
I'll pick you up in fifteen minutes."

Liddell glanced at the luminous face of the clock.
"Have you got rocks in your head? It's still the middle
of the night. Try me again in eight hours, baby."

"Johnny, the stables. They're burning and Blue
Queen is in there. Johnny, they've burned down the
stables."

Liddell was suddenly wide awake and ice cold.
"You're sure?"

"Connie just called me. He says it's a total loss."

"I'll be waiting for you down front, baby. Don't
stop to dress." He tossed the receiver back on its hook,
started stuffing his legs into his pants. He was standing out front of his apartment when Elsie Grant

braked the big convertible to a stop at the curb.

Conversation was held to a minimum as the girl expertly guided the car north to the 59th Street Bridge over onto Long Island. Less than an hour after he had received the call, she pulled the car into the parking lot beyond the stables.

Three companies of volunteer firemen were fighting what was left of the blaze. The uprights of the barns stood bare against the sky like the meatless ribs of some prehistoric monster. The air was heavy with the sickening-sweet odor of burning flesh. A small knot of men and women in varying degrees of undress stood at a distance watching the firemen put the finishing touches to the blaze.

Elsie tugged at Liddell's sleeve. "There's Connie." She pointed to the shrunken figure of the old man standing apart from the rest of the crowd, his hands jammed into his pockets, his hat shoved on the back of his head. The redhead caught Liddell by the hand, led him over.

"Tough luck, Connie," Liddell commiserated. "Blue Queen?"

The old man shook his head. "Must have been in the back stall. We couldn't get to her. It spread too fast." He shook his head, rubbed his hand over his face. "And the big race is tomorrow."

Liddell's face was grim in the reflected light. "Maybe it might be an idea to have another talk with the Poet."

The old man caught him by the arm. "No sense you getting in any deeper than you are, boy. Elsie told me what you did for her. You've done enough."

"What are you going to do, Connie?" Elsie wanted to know. "You scratching the entry?"

The old man shook his head. "I never scratched the entry yet and I'm not doing it now. The Witt Stables entry runs." He patted her shoulder. "The Blue was the best, but Silver Queen was quite a horse in her day. We might still make it, we might still make it."

"She should have been destroyed years ago and you

know it," Elsie flared. "You run that entry and a lot of people will lose their money. Silver Queen won't have a chance."

"We're not scratching," the old man mumbled stubbornly. He turned on his heel, stalked away. "And we're not giving out the news that the Queen is in there. Not until we have to."

The redhead stared at the old man's back as he melted into the shadows. "You can't let him do it, Johnny. That's all the Poet wants him to do."

Liddell shook his head. "It's too late now, baby. The bets are in and Riker is shooting for the biggest killing in his career." His eyes narrowed as a big sedan skidded to a stop at the edge of the parking lot. "Speak of the devil!"

He watched while Riker, Mendy and the tired-eyed guard from the hotel piled out of the car, mixed with the crowd gaping at the still smoldering ruins.

"Wait here, baby," Liddell told the girl. "I want to have a little talk with the Poet."

The girl caught his arm. "Don't do anything crazy, Johnny. Nothing can undo what's done. It's his trick."

Liddell nodded glumly, walked over to where the Poet stood. "It doesn't take long for good news to travel."

Riker grinned at him. "Well, well. If it isn't the shamus." He nodded to the ruins of the stable. "I hear Blue Queen's still in there."

"I wouldn't know," Liddell growled. "I don't suppose you or your stooges know anything about that?"

The Poet looked hurt. "How could we? We spent the whole evening at the hotel. Besides, I hear it was an old lamp that got kicked over. Sad, isn't it?" He pulled a handkerchief from his hip pocket, touched the tip of his nose. "I suppose the Old Man will be scratching the entry?"

"If he has nothing but milk horses to run, the Witt entry will be at the post when the fifth race starts."

Riker shrugged. "Makes no difference to me whether he scratches or not. Without the Blue, he couldn't win. And we've covered every dollar with Dalmatia to win. Without the Blue, Dalmatia's a breeze." He turned to Mendy. "You got it all down on her?"

Mendy nodded happily. "All over the country. We'll make a real killing on this one. A real killing."

"Let's get back and push some more," the Poet suggested, "before the word gets out Blue Queen won't be running for Witt." He turned to the car, seemed to remember something, swung back to Liddell. "I'll be expecting you to make good that IOU, shamus. We've got a real good enforcer collecting for us. Not that I wouldn't like to give him the business—to give you the business." He chuckled. "Or maybe you'd like to make it double or nothing?"

8

Johnny Liddell fidgeted through the first three races, managed to pick a winner and place by the time the fourth had been called. He left his box, followed the crowds back to the paddock where the entries in the fifth race were being walked.

The paddock odds board listed a Witt entry but gossip had forced the price down to 5 to 1. Liddell looked around for Witt's familiar blue and white colors, failed to find either the old man or his horse. He ambled with the throng, listening to the rumors flying about the possibility of a Witt scratch.

"I wish Connie would scratch it," one bettor growled. "I had a bundle on it, figuring Blue Queen would be running. Now the rumor is the Blue didn't get out of that stable fire this morning. You hear that?"

His companion nodded glumly. "I heard."

Liddell spotted Marty Riker standing near the rail

talking to a jockey in red and yellow silks, the boy scheduled to be up on Dalmatia, the dark horse the Poet had been touting.

From the grandstand came the sounds of the fourth race getting under way. Liddell caught sight of Connie Witt coming out from a stable near the back of the paddock. The old man saw him, waved to him. Liddell walked over.

"Tough break, Connie," he commiserated. "Real tough."

The old man spat a stream of tobacco juice at the turf. "You get down on the entry?" he wanted to know. "Price's down to 5 to 1. The Poet's covering everything he can lay his hands on. Fire broke too late for the papers to carry much on it."

Liddell growled. "Yeah. He really ought to make a killing on this one."

"He'll make a killing, all right. Do me a favor. Get over there and get some money down on number seven. All you can lay your hands on."

"Seven? That's the entry. Without Blue Queen—"

"You haven't got much time," the old man mumbled.

Liddell stared at him for a moment, nodded. "Okay, Connie." He shouldered his way through the crowd studying the horses, walked over to where the Poet stood.

The Poet grinned at him. "Want to see a real horse, shamus?" He pointed to a big red horse, which was acting skittish. "Knows she's a winner already."

"What's the price on the Witt entry?"

The heavy eyebrows raised, making the sad eyes look sadder. "You mean you want a piece of dead horse?" There was a note of surprise in his voice. "I'll do you a special favor. Your note against $2,500."

"You got a bet," Liddell growled. "Give me a memo on it."

Riker frowned slightly, pulled a memo pad from his breast pocket, scribbled on it and handed it to

Liddell. "That's 15 gees and I'll be expecting it by tomorrow night. Right?"

Liddell nodded.

The Poet looked from him to Mendy who came hustling up, his face flushed. "I took all the lay-offs on the Witt entry and I laid plenty with Danny B. and the Bug and Charley Garris. We've got everything we can beg, borrow or steal riding with Dalmatia. She's a breeze."

Liddell grunted. "You better be able to back it up, Poet. I hear Danny B. and the Bug really have some enforcers."

The Poet looked unhappy momentarily, then brightened. "Don't worry. The big red is in, and—" He stared at the far stable where Connie Witt had opened the double door. "That—that blue. That's not the Queen, is it?"

Mendy stared for a moment, shook his head. "That's that dog the old man keeps alive. That Silver Queen. She couldn't—"

The loud speaker boomed for attention. It started listing the entries for the fifth. When it reached position Number 7, the announcer listed Blue Queen with Morty Weir up.

A rumble of excitement swelled up from the paddock. The crowd started pushing toward the big blue Connie Witt was leading into the exercise compound.

The Poet's sallow face went chalky. Frantically he tore his way through the crowd, clawing, pushing to get to the old man. Finally he reached the outer rim of the crowd, stared at the big horse with stricken eyes.

"Blue Queen?" he gasped.

The old man grinned at him. "Sure. Who were you expecting to run for me?"

"But she burned last night. I smelled her burning."

"That's wasn't the Queen. That was some horse meat I got for the dogs. Made a hell of a smell, didn't it?" He turned his back on the gambler, gave the jockey wearing his colors a boost into the saddle. "The only thing we've got to beat is Dalmatia, Morty. It should be a breeze."

The jockey nodded, started the big roan toward the starting gate. "A breeze, Mr. Witt."

The Poet stood watching the horse fall into line to parade onto the track. He grabbed at his collar as though it had gotten too tight. "Mendy. Lay off on Dalmatia. Lay off as fast as you can. Danny B., the Bug, anybody. We can't cover."

The sound of a bugle floated from the grandstand, the loudspeaker announced the running of the fifth. "It's too late," he groaned.

Liddell patted the Poet on the shoulder. "I hope you make your killing, Poet. It couldn't happen to a nicer guy."

The white-faced Poet shuddered. "Don't say that. Don't mention that word," he pleaded.

A Grave Matter!

The voice on the telephone had been full throated, husky; the kind that could raise goosepimples the length of a man's spine.

The moment Johnny Liddell laid eyes on the redhead, he knew the voice belonged. She was sprawled out, her hair a coppery tangle on the beige rug, her arm crooked over her head. The eyes that stared up at him were slightly slanted, half closed; her lips were parted, showing the perfection of her teeth. A loosely tied dressing gown gave ample evidence that the magnificence of her façade had needed no artificial assist.

She was redheaded, she was luscious, she was stacked.

She was also dead.

Johnny Liddell rolled his eyes up from the body to where Inspector Herlehy of Homicide stood watching him with no show of enthusiasm. The inspector chomped away at the ever-present wad of gum, bobbed his head.

"Okay. Suppose you let us in on your secret. How you always manage to find them before they get cold," he grunted.

Liddell stole a last look at the body, shook his head sadly. "What a waste of good material." He turned back to the man from homicide. "I had a telephone call from her. She asked me to meet her here at ten." He consulted his watch. "I was right on the nose, give or take a few minutes."

Herlehy bobbed his head, looked unconvinced. "But she didn't say what it was she wanted to talk to you about?"

Liddell grinned. "You must have my wire tapped."

"I suppose you don't even know who she was?" Herlehy exploded.

Liddell looked back to the redhead, watched while two men from the Photographic Unit took shots of the body from various angles. "She was a cigarette girl at the Café Martin. Called herself Leslie Carter." He waited while a man in a white jacket shoved a form in front of the inspector to be initialed. Behind them, two men from the Medical Examiner's office were transferring the body to a stretcher, strapping it on. Herlehy handed back the form, nodded for Liddell to continue. Johnny shrugged. "That's it. Her name was Leslie Carter. She called me, said she'd have something for me at ten."

"Johnny, if you're holding out—"

Liddell grimaced. "You know better than that, Inspector. If I had any idea of who killed her, or why, do you think I'd be standing here?" He bobbed his head in the direction of the door where the men from the M.E.'s office were wheeling the stretcher out. "I'd be out getting her someone to keep her company down at the morgue."

Herlehy scratched at the side of his jaw. "Larry Harris runs the Café Martin. You think he's mixed up in this?"

Liddell shrugged. "Why don't you ask him?"

"I intend to," the inspector grunted. He squinted at Liddell. "As long as you don't know what the girl wanted to see you about, I guess you won't be sticking your nose into this one?"

"That depends, Inspector."

"On what?"

Liddell shrugged. "My guess is whoever killed her did it because they were afraid she was going to spill something to me. Maybe they'll figure she might have told me more than she did. In that case, they might have some ideas about shutting me up, too." He grinned glumly. "If that's the case, you couldn't expect me to just stand by, could you?"

The inspector started to explode, settled for a red flush that ran up his neck from his collar. "Just make sure you don't give them any ideas in that direction," he ordered. "This is a murder, and murder's a police business."

"Unless it happens to be my murder. I get real sensitive about that." Liddell nodded to the white-haired man, turned and headed for the door.

Herlehy stared after him, expressed some highly censorable opinions about private detectives in general and Johnny Liddell in particular.

The Café Martin was a cellar club on Heather Mews in Greenwich Village. It was headquarters for the weirdos and exhibitionists who performed nightly for the tourists and sensation seekers who travel downtown to marvel at the way the Other Half lives and loves. A short flight of stairs led down into a large subterranean room that had been made by knocking out the walls of three adjoining cellars. The only lighting was provided by the stubs of candles stuck in the necks of wine bottles; a perpetual cloud of smoke swirled lazily near the ceiling.

Mobiles spun in the smoky air and customers enjoyed the proceedings from canvas chairs, while waitresses with long, dank hair and dangling earrings worked their way through the chairs, their swaying hips brushing lightly against the customers.

Johnny Liddell walked down the short flight of stairs from the sidewalk level and stood in the doorway looking around. In the far corner of the room, a shaggy type in black beret, shapeless slacks and sport shirt was reading some German verse with comically extreme gestures. Sitting at his feet, a bearded young man was pounding unmelodiously on a pair of bongos.

One of the long-haired waitresses materialized at his side. "Alone, Pops?"

Liddell nodded. "Harris around?"

The long-haired girl lost interest. She nodded toward the rear of the room. "Back in the office." She glided off into the dimness.

Liddell worked his way through the chairs, grinned at the snatches of "authentic beat" that was flying around to give the tourists something to talk about on their way back to the sticks. Joints like the Café Martin, created strictly for the tourist trade, are as much a part of the Village as the tearooms that squat cheek to jowl next to the dives that keep the vice squad working a full schedule, the art galleries, the gift shops and the bookstores that pander to the artistic element.

In the rear of the room, Liddell rapped his knuckles against the door marked *Private*. Without waiting for an answer, he pushed it open, walked in.

Larry Harris looked up from the open ledger on which he was working, scowled when he recognized Johnny Liddell. A heavy-set man with the face of an unsuccessful club fighter, his ears two twisted lumps of flesh stuck to the side of a totally bald head, studied the newcomer disinterestedly.

"What do you want, shamus?" the man behind the desk growled. Larry Harris was an old-timer. The lean wolfishness of his face had been blurred by an overlay of fat over the years, but flat, lusterless, lethal eyes still peered from under heavily veined, thickened eyelids.

Liddell walked in, closed the door behind him. "I dropped by to offer my condolences. Or didn't you know your cigarette girl was murdered?"

Larry Harris leaned back in his chair. "So what's it to you?"

"Just before she was murdered, she called me. Asked me to meet her at her place at ten."

"So what's that to me?"

"I thought you might like to know what she called me about."

There was a slight flicker of interest in the lusterless eyes. It died away almost as fast as it came. "Why should I want to know?" He pulled a cigarette holder from his breast pocket, started to screw a cigarette into it. His eyes rolled up from the holder to Liddell. "Maybe it's better I don't know. Knowing what she did got real fatal for her. Maybe that's what happens to anybody who knows." He tilted the cigarette holder from the corner of his mouth. "So, if that's what you came here to tell me—"

"I came here to tell you that I'm taking cards in the game. The redhead came to me for protection, someone hit her. That hurts my pride." Liddell grinned glumly. "I figure it's only fair to give you warning, Larry." He put the flat of his hands on the desk, leaned across to the man sitting behind it. "Because if I find out you had anything to do with what happened to her, I'm coming for you."

Larry Harris sneered. Without taking his eyes off Liddell's face, he turned his head to the man with the bulky shoulders. "Throw him out, Mike. He's beginning to annoy me."

The man with the battered face screwed his features into what passed for a grin. He reached up, slipped out his denture, dropped it into his pocket. He started around the desk in an odd, shuffling motion.

Liddell straightened up, watched the big man's approach warily. Mike moved with a speed surprising in a man his size. He slammed a beefy fist at Liddell's head, took a sharp right to the midsection in return. The big man roared like a stung bear, started boring in again. He caught Liddell on the side of the head with a hamlike fist that started bells ringing. Sensing his advantage, the big man threw caution to the winds, came in flailing with both fists.

Liddell backed away from the attack, side-stepped. He caught the big man under the right ear with a blow that carried his full strength. Mike staggered back, a dazed expression on his face. Liddell planted his right to the elbow in the big man's midsection. As the bodyguard folded over, Liddell brought up his knee, caught him in the face. There was a crunching sound as Mike's nose broke again. Liddell chopped down at the exposed back of the big man's neck. He hit the floor face first, didn't move.

Liddell looked from the fallen man to the man behind the desk. Larry Harris sat glaring his hatred, his hand in a half-opened drawer. Liddell grinned at him. "Still coppering your bets, eh Larry?" He nodded toward the hand in the drawer. "In the old days you used to do a lot better when you did your own dirty work. Maybe you ought to go back to doing your own muscle work. You can't depend on these meatballs. They're all soft inside."

He stepped across the unconscious man's body, headed for the door. As soon as the door had closed behind him, Larry Harris reached for his phone, started dialing a number. When he was finished with his call, he got up, picked up a water carafe, spilled it over the bodyguard, brought him sputtering back to consciousness.

A little after midnight, Johnny Liddell strolled aimlessly down the street where Leslie Carter had lived. The shades were drawn on all the front windows. Aside from a few cars that shot by, there was no sign of life along the street.

When he had satisfied himself that the uniformed patrolman stationed outside the house had been withdrawn, Liddell flipped his cigarette into the gutter, started across the street. He headed up the short flight of stairs to the vestibule. A row of letterboxes supplied the information that while Leslie Carter had lived in 2A, the other apartment on that floor was occupied by Flora Winters. He pushed open the hall door, headed for the stairs.

On the second landing, he walked past the door to Leslie Carter's apartment, knocked on the door on which was stenciled 2B.

After a moment, the door opened, a tall blonde stood in the opening. "Yes?"

"Flora Winters?"

"That's right." The light was behind the girl, Liddell couldn't see her features. "Who are you?"

"My name's Liddell. I'm a detective."

There was a trace of annoyance in the girl's voice. "I've already answered enough questions to last me a lifetime, let alone a nighttime." She started to close the door.

"I'm not with the police. I'm a private detective."

"All the more reason."

Liddell put his foot in the doorway. "Leslie Carter called me just before she was killed. She wanted me to help her."

The blonde paused, then pulled the door. "Oh, all right. Come on in." She waited until he had accepted the invitation, closed the door after him. She was wearing a dressing gown that clung closely to a figure that was obviously worth clinging to. Her thick, glossy blond hair was caught just above her ear with a bright blue ribbon, then allowed to cascade down over her shoulders. Swelling breasts showed at the V-neck of the gown, a thin waist hinted at full hips, long legs.

She eyed Liddell curiously. "Why come to me?"

Liddell shrugged. "You lived next door to her. I thought you might know if she was in any kind of a jam."

The blonde considered, shook her head. "She didn't talk much." She walked over to the couch, dropped onto it, the gown revealed long, shapely legs as she crossed them.

Liddell looked at the legs.

"I don't suppose you saw her visitor or visitors earlier tonight?"

Flora Winters shook her head. "This isn't the kind of a neighborhood where you keep track of your neighbor." She reached out to a coffee table with devastating effect on the neckline of the gown. "I suppose you know that I was instrumental in getting her the job?" She leaned back, jutted her breasts against the fragile fabric of the gown, put her cigarette in the corner of her mouth.

Liddell shook his head, provided a light. "Then you know Larry Harris?"

The blonde made a move of distaste. "I don't think that's the right word. I'm acquainted with him because we're both in business here in the Village." She leaned forward for the light, drew a mouthful of smoke, let it dribble from between half-parted lips. "I run an antique shop on the Mews—a few doors down from the Café Martin."

Liddell held the burning match a moment too long, scorched his finger, snapped it out with a scowl. "How did Leslie Carter come into it?"

The girl on the couch shrugged. "She was out of work. I happened to hear that the Café Martin had an opening for a cigarette girl. She went down, got the job. Simple as that." She studied Liddell from under carefully tinted lids. "I should imagine that investigating a murder would be the job of the police, though. You must have more of an interest in it than just the fact that she called you."

Liddell considered, grunted. "I have a feeling that because she made that telephone call, she was murdered. Was she the type that might be putting pressure on anybody?"

-"I wouldn't know. I just knew her as a neighbor. I had no business dealings with her." The blonde eyed him curiously. "You think the killer was in the room with her when she called you?"

"It figures." Liddell stared around the apartment, noted for the first time that most of the furnishings were far more expensive than would be expected in such a neighborhood. His eyes came back to the blonde. "Were you home around the time she was killed?"

The blonde smiled at him. "Nobody has told me what time she was killed." She squinted as a thin plume of smoke curled upward from the cigarette, stung her eyes. "But I have been home since around eight."

Liddell nodded. "She called me at about 8:45." He scowled, stared at the walls. "She was shot. You didn't hear a thing, huh?"

Flora Winters shook her head. "The walls are thin, but you'll notice my walls are hung with tapestries. They act as soundproofing as well as being decorative." She took the cigarette from between her lips, studied the carmined end. "I'm afraid it's just as I told you, Mr. Liddell. There's nothing I can tell you." She rolled her eyes up from the cigarette to Johnny's face, smiled coldly. "And it is getting rather late."

"Real subtle," Liddell nodded. "But I think I get the point."

The following morning, Johnny Liddell was already at his desk when the redheaded secretary came in. She opened the door to the private office, stared at him with undisguised surprise.

"What goes? You turning over a new leaf, or haven't you been home yet?"

Liddell looked up from a pile of folders he'd been studying, scowled at her. "Just checking on what time you get the office open." He leaned back. "How many assignments we got on our open file, Pinky?"

Pinky pursed her lips, counted off on her fingers. "The Fineman wedding in Great Neck. You have Williams and Gannett out there guarding the coffeepots—"

Liddell nodded for her to continue.

"The Wellman divorce bit. But that's practically washed up. All we have left is to itemize the evidence and send the bill."

"That wouldn't be it."

Pinky frowned at him. "What are you looking for?"

"A girl called me last night, said she had some evidence in a case I was working on. Two hours later, she's dead." He scowled at the redhead in the doorway. "What case?"

Pinky shook her head. "The only other thing on the books is the Seaway Insurance retainer. There's no case there. Just the retainer." She ridged her forehead in thought, shook her head. "Nothing."

Liddell got up from his chair, walked to the window, looked down into Bryant Park eight stories below. "Just the same, someone thought she had something that we'd be interested in. They thought enough of it to kill her to keep her from spilling." He turned, walked to the desk, started dialing.

"What are you going to do?" the redhead wanted to know.

"I'm going to find out what Seaway has on the fire that might be hot enough to cause someone to kill her."

Johnny Liddell left the elevator on the 54th floor of the Chrysler Building, walked down the corridor to the double glass door bearing the inscription *Seaway Indemnity Company*. He pushed through the door into the ante-room, walked up to the receptionist's desk.

"Lee Devon. My name's Johnny Liddell. I'm expected."

The girl smiled brightly, nodded. When she got up, she was taller than he'd thought, the black knit dress clung to her ample curves as she headed for an inner door. "Will you walk this way, please?"

Liddell watched the soft play of her hips against the knitted dress. "I just don't have the equipment, honey," he smiled.

The girl gave no sign she had heard, held the door for him. He could smell the expensive perfume she wore, had the impression of a well-rounded hip as he squeezed past her into the inner room.

Lee Devon got up from behind the highly polished desk set between two windows at the far end of the room and met Liddell with an outstretched hand. "I'm glad you came by, Johnny. Real glad." His handshake was firm and cordial.

"Something?" Liddell asked.

Devon waited until the girl had closed the door behind her on her way out. "Maybe, maybe not." He looked worried. "If there is something, it's a real screwy setup." He led the way back to the desk, indicated a chair to Johnny, walked around to his own desk chair. "After you called, I did a double check on everything we've handled in the past year. Everything is clean and above board. Not an indication of anything phony."

Liddell looked disappointed. "But—"

"Nothing phony," Devon reiterated. "But there is something that has been bugging me a little." He opened his top drawer, took out three paper folders. "In the past two years, we've had a couple of real expensive fire claims." He indicated the files. "I've had the reports pulled out. In every case we've paid off."

"But?"

Devon opened the top file, brought out some glossies, flattened them out on the top of his desk. "Take a look here." He indicated one of the glossies with a pencil. "This was the Dunstan house on Sands Point. You can see how heavy the flames were. A complete loss."

Liddell eyed the charred timbers, the blackened remains of the walls, nodded. "So?"

"See the intensity of the flame near this wall?" The tip of the pencil rested on a heavily charred area. "That was in the living room." He selected another glossy, pointed to a similarly charred area. "Here's another point of equal intensity. This was in the den." He looked up at Liddell. "In an accidental fire, there's one starting point, then the fire spreads. It's obvious that this one started simultaneously in those two places."

"You think the place was torched?"

The insurance adjuster leaned back in his chair. "That's what's so puzzling about it, Johnny. The Dunstans have more money than they'll ever need. And besides, they were careless with their insurance. The house and its contents weren't insured for anything near to worth."

Liddell pursed his lips. "And the others?"

Devon shrugged. "Not quite as much physical evidence of a torching, but all of them complete losses." He grimaced. "All owned by people above suspicion, none of them insured for enough to make it worth anybody's while." He leaned forward, replaced the photos in the file. "We had a conference with the home office people, decided to pay off the claims, so there's never been any action taken."

Liddell walked over to where a water cooler stood humming to itself against the wall, helped himself to a cup of water. He drained the cup, crushed it into a ball, tossed it at the waste basket.

"There's nothing else that the girl who called me might have a line on?"

Devon shook his head.

Liddell shrugged. "Maybe I'm off on the wrong track. Maybe she had some information about Old Man Wellman that would help his wife's divorce case or—"

Lee Devon's forehead was ridged with a frown that etched a V between his eyes. "Except for one thing, Johnny. After you called, I did some checking around. A few days ago, the office had a call. It was a woman. She wanted to know who did our investigations. My assistant gave her your name and office number."

Johnny Liddell looked grim. "In that case, mind if I have a look at those files?"

"Be my guest." Lee Devon pushed a button on the side of his phone. "I'll get you an office where you won't be disturbed."

The door to the reception room opened, the girl in the knit dress stepped in. "Yes, Mr. Devon?"

"Find an empty office for Johnny, Miss Grant. If there's anything he wants, see that he gets it." His eyes rolled from the girl to Liddell. "That is, within reason."

Johnny Liddell rubbed his eyes, closed the last of the insurance adjustment files. The ash tray at his elbow was almost filled, his coat was draped over the back of his chair, the knot of his tie at half mast. He looked up as the door opened, the girl from the reception desk walked in, placed two containers of coffee on the desk.

"You like it black or regular?" She indicated the container with an X scribbled on the cover. "That's the black."

Liddell reached over, snagged the container. He indicated a chair. "Sit down. No use of the coffee going to waste."

The girl grinned at him. "I didn't intend it to." She drew up a chair, picked up the other container. "How you coming?"

Liddell raked at his hair with clenched fingers, shook his head. "I'm not sure." He gouged the top out of the coffee container. "I've got a sneaking hunch. But that's all it is right now, a hunch." He took a sip from the container, burned his tongue, swore softly. "But it's the only way that anything makes sense."

"Do you any good to talk it out?"

"It might. I—" He broke off. "I can't just call you Hey, you. You got a name?"

"Charley."

Liddell's eyebrows raised. "Charley?"

"My father's private joke. My full name's Charlene. But everybody calls me Charley." She lifted the top from her coffee container, swirled the contents around slowly. "Any other questions?"

"That'll do for now." Liddell tried his coffee again, managed to swallow a mouthful without scalding himself. "You familiar with the Dunstan case and the others?"

Charley shrugged. "Generally. As part-time secretary for Mr. Devon, I get to hear something of what goes on in Adjustment. For a while there it looked like we weren't going to pay off on the Dunstan claim. But when it turned out that the Dunstans were in Europe when it happened, and the claim didn't even cover the loss—" She shrugged. "They decided to drop it."

"Figuring?" Liddell asked.

The girl sipped at her coffee. "Tramps or somebody staying in the house got careless. Something like that."

Liddell indicated the files on his desk. "Could you run me off a list of all the items lost in these fires?"

"When do you need it?"

Liddell shrugged. "As soon as I can get it."

The girl managed to look unhappy. "I'll have to stay tonight to finish it. Could you drop back to pick it up tonight?"

"I don't know what time I'll be free. Let's make it at your place. Then you won't have to hang around."

The girl grinned at him. "That's downright considerate of you."

He picked up the pile of folders, handed it across to her. "Maybe you'd better get started." He consulted his watch. "I've got some checking to do that'll take most of the afternoon."

Charley took the files, gave him an indignant look, hightailed it out of the room. Liddell grinned as she slammed the door behind her. He consulted the intercom directory on the desk, dialed 243.

After a moment, Lee Devon's voice came through the phone.

"Liddell, Lee. Can you check the cross files with the other companies, get me a list of all fires in the past six months and a breakdown of the most valuable items lost?"

"You on to something?"

"Could be."

There was a worried note in the voice on the other end. "Don't forget, Johnny. We backed away from any action on this because the people involved were important. Don't get us into anything we can't handle."

"You know me, Lee."

"Yeah, I know you. That's what I'm worrying about."

"How long will it take you to get all the information?"

There was a slight pause. "A couple of days, maybe."

Liddell grunted. "It'll have to do. But the sooner, the better."

Charlene Grant, Lee Devon's receptionist, lived on East 61st Street, a block of brownstone houses that had the distinction of having the only trees left in that part of the East Side. They were dwarfed and stunted from exposure to the grime, gas fumes and lack of sun that are part and parcel of the New York scene. But they were trees.

The cab dropped Johnny Liddell in front of one of the brownstones which nestled anonymously in the row, he climbed to the vestibule, pushed the button under the name Charlene Grant. There was a stuttering of the latch, he pushed the inner door open and walked into the hall. Charlene appeared silhouetted in the open door to the apartment on first floor rear.

"Down here."

Liddell followed her into the apartment, tossed his hat at a table. "Finished?"

Charley nodded, indicated a list on the coffee table. He walked over, picked it up, glanced through it, nodded his satisfaction. "Great." He sat on the arm of an upholstered chair, took inventory of her obvious assets. "You really want to help me with this one?"

The girl nodded enthusiastically, then with a cautious afterthought, "It won't involve typing?"

Liddell grinned, shook his head. "I know where there's a job for a good looker as a cigarette girl—" He waved off an interruption. "I'll fix it with Devon. You interested?"

The girl considered, bobbed her head. "Could be." She walked over to a portable bar near the wall, held up a bottle of Scotch for approval. "Drink?"

Liddell nodded. "On the rocks." He watched while she dumped some ice into the glass, spilled Scotch over it. "This could be dangerous."

Charley cocked an eye at him. "Drinking with you?"

"Working as a cigarette girl." He accepted the glass she brought him. "I want somebody in the Café Martin who can keep an eye on Larry Harris. If he were to find out it was a plant—"

"He won't." She held up her glass. "Here's to the new cigarette girl at the Café Martin." She took a deep sip from the glass, gave him the full effect of her slanted green eyes over the rim.

Liddell consulted his watch. "It's almost seven now. Harris doesn't usually show up at the cafe until around twelve."

The girl walked over to the couch, dropped onto it. She patted the pillow at her side. "That'll give you more time to tell me what I'm supposed to do." She pouted when he showed no signs of walking over to the couch. "Sit over here by me. I won't hurt you."

She didn't.

The man behind the desk in the back room of the Café Martin laced his fingers at the back of his head, let his eyes roam from the top of Charlene Grant's head to her ballet shod feet with appropriate stops in between.

"What makes you think we can use a cigarette girl here at the Café Martin, baby?" Larry Harris wanted to know.

Charley shrugged. "I read the papers. The one who used to work here is dead. You need somebody to replace her." She shrugged again. "I'm applying for the job."

Larry Harris nodded, the heavily veined lids half veiling his eyes. "You live with your folks, baby?"

The girl shook her head. "This is just a breather until I get my break. I came here from Oswego to go on the stage." She grinned shamefacedly. "But in the meantime, a girl's got to eat."

Harris got up from his chair, walked around the

desk. "I happen to know a lot of people in that racket. I might be able to help you."

"That'd be awful nice of you."

"Think nothing of it. I like to do things for people who are nice to me. It's like I always say—"

A door in the rear of the office opened, a tall blonde stepped in. "Oh, I'm sorry. I didn't mean to interrupt—"

Larry Harris straightened up, dropped his hand from Charley's arm. "Think nothing of it. I was just putting on a new cigarette girl." He patted Charlene, winked to her. "Go on out front, baby. The kid in the checkroom will get you a uniform, show you the ropes."

Flora Winters waited until Charlene had left, then she whirled on Harris. "You crazy? I told you not to get so friendly with the help. Didn't you learn anything at all from what happened with that other little tramp?"

"Take it easy." Harris stiff-legged it around the desk, dropped into his chair. "Maybe you think it's smart waltzing in here like this? Okay, so it's just some kid I'm putting on. Suppose it was the cops in here?"

The blonde narrowed her eyes at him. "You're supposed to keep that door locked if there's anyone in here. When it's open it means the coast is clear. Or did you forget?"

The man behind the desk looked sulky. "I still think there's too much cloak and dagger. Why can't you just phone and—"

"Because wires can be tapped," Flora snapped. She opened her handbag, pulled out a batch of pages torn from a magazine. "I've got a job for you."

Harris looked unhappy. "So soon?"

The blonde ignored him, smoothed out the pages of the magazine. "This should be a cinch. It's on Manhasset Bay, about 20 miles out. House is owned by Vincent Derby, a ceramics collector. He has some pieces I can place right away. Should be worth twenty thousand or more and I don't think there's a chance they could be traced."

Greed clashed with caution on the man's face. He finally leaned over, studied the magazine article. "Article says he has some Ming vases that are worth a fortune—"

"He has a lot of things, but some of them are traceable. They're no good to us. I'll tell you what to take. We take that and nothing more." There was a snap to the woman's voice. "I've done all right for both of us up to now. We'll continue to do it my way."

"When do we do the job?"

The blonde shrugged. "That's your department. You make the arrangements, let me know when you're ready. I want to go along and pick out the pieces myself."

Larry Harris bobbed his head glumly. "I'll have one of the boys ride out there in the morning and case the place. We should be ready by the end of the week."

The blonde stiffened, put her fingers to her lips, indicated for the man to keep talking. He frowned, nodded, kept talking as the woman walked to the door and pulled it open.

Charley Grant stood on the other side. The blonde caught her by the arm, pulled her into the room.

Charley made an effort to regain her balance, but the blonde slammed the door, was all over her. She slashed at her face with the flat of her hand, backhanded it into position. Charley tried to fight back, but the blonde's earlier advantage overwhelmed her. She was slammed back against the wall, slid to a sitting position, buried her face in her hands.

Flora looked from the girl on the floor to the man behind the desk, her breast heaving. "You satisfied? She was a plant!"

"By who?"

"How do I know?" the blonde gasped. "My guess would be that keyhole peeper, Liddell." She nodded to the girl. "Get her into a chair."

Harris picked the girl up, dumped her into a chair. Her head rolled forward. "She's passed out."

"She's faking," Flora snarled. She picked up the carafe of water, splashed it in Charley's face. The girl shook her head, wiped her face with the flat of her hand. For a moment it was difficult for her to focus her eyes. When she did, she made an effort to get out of the chair, was pushed back roughly by the woman.

"Who sent you?"

Charley shook her head. She was dimly aware that the woman's hand was flashing toward her in an arc, felt the impact as it connected. Flora hit her again, but Charley had the sensation it was happening to some-body else. A spreading black pool mercifully swirled over her and she sank into its depths.

"That won't do any good," Harris growled. "She's passed out again."

"Tie her up. We'll take her with us on the Manhas-set job."

Harris gasped. "You planning on going ahead with it?"

Flora bobbed her head. "It may be our last job for a long while. But we're not passing up that kind of money." She indicated the girl. "As for her, when they investigate the fire, they'll just find her bones. They'll mark her down as somebody who crawled in for shelter, set fire to the place with a cigarette or something."

Johnny Liddell stood huddled in the doorway across from the Café Martin, smoked his fifth cigarette to a butt, dropped it to the ground, crushed it out. He started across the street, walked down the short flight of stairs to the Café Martin. He crossed to the coat-check cubicle. "Where's your cigarette girl?"

"Don't you read the papers, Pops? She's dead. And if she isn't, they're playing her a dirty trick. They're burying her tomorrow."

"What about the new one?"

The girl shrugged. "No new one, Pops. You tell me your brand—"

Liddell swore under his breath. He pushed his way through the tables, headed for the door marked *Private*. As he shoved the door open, he tugged the .45 from his shoulder holster.

Inside the room, Larry Harris and his bodyguard looked up, stared at the .45 in Liddell's fist. Harris looked from Liddell to Mike and back. "What do you want?"

"You, pal. Boiled, fried or roasted I want you."

Harris tossed another look at his bodyguard. Mike started toward Liddell, Johnny swung the barrel of the .45 in a small arc, laid it across Mike's mouth. The big man stumbled backwards, got his legs tangled in a low stool, crashed to the floor in its wreckage.

Harris used that moment to go for the gun in his drawer, froze with his fingers touching the barrel as the .45 covered him again. "Where's Charlene Grant?" Liddell walked over to where Harris sat, caught a handful of his hair, pulled his head back. "Where is she?" When the man in the chair didn't answer, Liddell bared his teeth in a mirthless grin. "You're going to talk, Harris. Or so help me, I'll leave you as toothless as the day you were born."

The man in the chair licked at his lips. When Liddell lifted the barrel of the .45, Harris cringed back. "In the back of the antique shop. The Winter's dame. She's the one you want. Not me. Get her and you'll have all the answers you need."

Flora Winters stood, arms crossed, watching Charley Grant struggling to regain consciousness. "A real smart girl, weren't you? Liddell figured by planting you on Harris he'd get something, huh?" She pushed Charley's head back as it rolled on her chest. "Well, suspecting something and proving something may be two different things."

The girl in the chair opened her eyes, managed to focus them on the blonde. She licked at her lips, tried to talk. Her voice was a hoarse croak.

Suddenly the back door to the shop shot open, Johnny Liddell sent Harris sprawling in. He landed on his hands and knees, stayed there. The blonde took in the situation in a glance. Quickly she moved to the girl in the chair, put a gun to the side of her head.

"Drop your gun, Liddell. Or I'll pull this trigger. Drop it."

Liddell debated, correctly interpreted the look in the woman's eyes, tossed his .45 into the room. "You can't get away with it. They'll nail you for killing Leslie Carter."

The blonde shook her head. "No. When they find you dead and Harris with your bullet in him, I'll tell them how you nailed Harris and he tried to shoot it out. Neither of you made it." She smiled. "But I'll be a witness to how bravely you went out."

Liddell scowled. "You'd kill your own partner, too?"

"He's no more use to me. I—"

"You can't get both of us, baby," a voice from behind her growled.

Liddell looked past her to see the man on the floor pull a knife from his pocket, catch the blade between thumb and forefinger. The blonde's eyes jumped from Liddell to the other man. She swung the gun, squeezed the trigger frantically. The first slug hit Harris at almost the same instant the knife left his fingers. He fell over backwards.

Liddell turned. The blonde stood facing him. The handle of the knife protruded from her abdomen like some obscene horn. She dropped her gun, wrapped both hands around the handle of the knife, tried to tug it free. She swayed for a moment, toppled to the ground.

She was dead when Liddell turned her over.

Inspector Herlehy looked from Johnny Liddell to Charley Grant, shook his head. "You took stupid chances," he growled. "But you walk away from it smelling of roses." He consulted a flimsy on his desk. "A check of Flora Winters's inventory and her sales records show most of the valuables lost in the fires went through her shop."

Charley Grant shook her head. "That's the way Johnny said it worked. But where'd they get the nerve to sell it so openly?"

"Why not?" Liddell wanted to know. "Everybody took for granted the stuff was burned up in the fires, the insurance people paid off, the people who wanted the stuff asked no questions. It was a real safe racket."

"Not so safe," Herlehy told him. "Flora Winters and her right-hand man are playing three-handed pinochle with Leslie Carter right now."

"But why'd they kill her?" Charley wanted to know.

Liddell shrugged. "She wanted in. She stumbled on what they were doing, tried to blackmail Flora. To show she had aces, she called me right in front of Flora." He turned back to Herlehy. "One of the things that bugged me was that those walls were paper thin. Yet nobody heard the shot. It wasn't until I got into Flora's apartment and saw the soundproof draperies on the walls that I figured how it happened." He caught Charley by the elbow, lifted her to her feet. "Let's get going, Charley. You need some sleep."

"Sleep?" Herlehy wanted to know.

Liddell considered, shrugged with a grin. He followed the girl to the door, winked at the man behind the desk, closed the door behind them.